CONFLICT ON AERLITH

Trackers, Weaponeers, Heavy Troopers, Giants—once they might have been men, before the very essence of their genetic structure had been twisted and shaped to make of them a race of slave warriors.

Termagants, Fiends, Long-horned Murderers, Blue Horrors, Juggers—a thousand generations ago they might have been Basics, members of the reptilian race that had all but driven mankind into extinction.

Now, on an all-but-forgotten world on the edge of infinity, man and lizard meet in final battle in a story by one of the finest writers of our generation!

THE DRAGON-MASTERS

JACK VANCE

SF
ace books
A Division of Charter Communications Inc.
A GROSSET & DUNLAP COMPANY
51 Madison Avenue
New York, New York 10010

An ACE Book

This Ace printing: December 1981
Published Simultaneously in Canada
2 4 6 8 0 9 7 5 3 1
Manufactured in the United States of America

THE DRAGONMASTERS

CHAPTER 1

THE APARTMENTS of Joaz Banbeck, carved deep from the heart of a limestone crag, consisted of five principal chambers, on five different levels. At the top were the relinquarium and a formal council chamber: the first a room of somber magnificence housing the various archives, trophies and mementos of the Banbecks; the second a long narrow hall, with dark wainscoting chest-high and a white plaster vault above, extending the entire width of the drag, so that balconies overlooked Banbeck Vale at one end and Kergan's Way at the other.

Below were Joaz Banbeck's private quarters: a parlor and bedchamber, then next his study and finally, at the bottom, a workroom where Joaz permitted none but himself.

Entry to the apartments was through the study, a large L-shaped room with an elaborate groined ceiling, from which depended four garnet-encrusted chandeliers. These were now dark; into the room came only a watery gray light from four honed glass plates on which, in the manner of a *camera obscura*, were focused views across Banbeck Vale. The walls were paneled with lignified reed; a rug patterned in angles, squares and circles of maroon, brown and black covered the floor.

In the middle of the study stood a naked man, his only covering the long fine brown hair which flowed down his back, the golden torc which clasped his neck. His features were sharp and angular, his body thin; he appeared to be listening, or perhaps meditating. Occasionally he glanced at a yellow marble globe on a nearby shelf, whereupon his lips would move, as if he were committing to memory some phrase or sequence of ideas.

At the far end of the study a heavy door eased open. A flower-faced young woman peered through, her expression mischievous, arch. At the sight of the naked man, she clapped her hands to her mouth, stifling a gasp. The naked man turned, but the heavy door had already swung shut.

For a moment he stood deep in frowning reflection, then slowly went to the wall on the inside leg of the L. He swung out a section of the bookcase, passed through the opening, and behind him the bookcase thudded shut. Descending a spiral staircase he came out into a chamber roughhewn from the rock: Joaz Banbeck's private workroom. A bench supported tools, metal shapes and fragments, a bank of electromotive cells, oddments of circuitry: the current objects of Joaz Banbeck's curiosity.

The naked man glanced at the bench, picked up one of the devices, inspected it with something like condescension, though his gaze was as clear and wondering as that of a child. Muffled voices from the study penetrated to the workroom. The naked man raised his head to listen, then stooped under the bench. He lifted a block of stone, slipped through the gap into a dark void. Replacing the stone, he took up a luminous wand, and set off down a narrow tunnel, which presently dipped to join a natural cavern. At irregular intervals luminous tubes exuded a wan light, barely enough to pierce the murk. The naked man jogged forward swiftly, the silken hair flowing like a nimbus behind him.

Back in the study the minstrel-maiden Phade and an elderly seneschal were at odds. "Indeed I saw him!" Phade insisted. "With these two eyes of mine, one of the sacerdotes, standing thus and so, as I have described." She tugged angrily at his elbow. "Do you think me bereft of my wits, or hysterical?"

Rife, the seneschal, shrugged, committing himself neither one way nor the other. "I do not see him now." He climbed the staircase, peered into the sleeping parlor. "Empty. The doors above are bolted." He peered owlishly at Phade. "And I sat at my post in the entry."

"You sat sleeping. Even when I came past you snored!"

"You are mistaken; I did but cough."

"With your eyes closed, your head lolling back?"

Rife shrugged once more. "Asleep or awake, it is all the same. Admitting that the creature gained access, how did he leave? I was wakeful after you summoned me, as you must agree."

"Then remain on guard, while I find Joaz Banbeck." Phade ran down the passage which presently joined Bird Walk, so called for the series of fabulous birds of lapis, gold, cinnabar, malachite and marcasite in-laid into the marble. Through an arcade of green and gray jade in spiral columns she passed out into Kergan's Way, a natural defile which formed the main thoroughfare of Banbeck Village. Reaching the portal she summoned a pair of lads from the fields. "Run to the brooder, find Joaz Banbeck! Hasten, bring him here; I must speak with him."

The boys ran off toward a low cylinder of black brick a mile to the north.

Phade waited. With the sun Skene at its nooning, the air was warm; the fields of vetch, bellegarde, spharganum, gave off a pleasant odor. Phade went to lean against a fence. Now she began to wonder about the urgency of her news, even its basic reality. "No!" she told herself fiercely. "I saw! I saw!"

At either side tall white cliffs rose to Banbeck Verge, with mountains and crags beyond, and span-ning all the dark sky flecked with feathers of cirrus. Skene glittered dazzling bright, a finuscule flake of brilliance.

Phade sighed, half-convinced of her own mistake. Once more, less vehemently, she reassured herself. Never before had she seen a sacerdote; why should she imagine one now?

The boys, reaching the brooder, had disappeared into the dust of the exercise pens. Scales gleamed and winked; grooms, dragon masters, armorers in black leather moved about their work. After a mo-ment Joaz Banbeck came into view. He mounted a tall thin-legged Spider, urged it to the full extent of its head-jerking lope, pounded down the track toward Banbeck Village.

Phade's uncertainty grew. Might Joaz become exasperated? Would he dismiss her news with an unbelieving stare? Uneasily she watched his approach. Coming to Banbeck Vale only a month before she still felt unsure of her status. Her preceptors had trained her diligently in the barren little valley to the south where she had been born, but the disparity between teaching and practical reality at times bewildered her. She had learned that all men obeyed a small and identical group of behaviors; Joaz Banbeck, however, observed no such limits, and Phade found him completely unpredictable.

She knew him to be a relatively young man, though his appearance provided no guide to his age. He had a pale austere face in which gray eyes shone like crystals, a long thin mouth which suggested flexibility, yet never curved far from a straight line. He moved languidly; his voice carried no vehemence; he made no pretense of skill with either saber or pistol. He seemed deliberately to shun any gesture which might win the admiration or affection of his subjects. Phade originally had thought him cold, but presently changed her mind. He was, so she decided, a man bored and lonely, with a quiet humor which at times seemed rather grim. But he treated her without discourtesy, and Phade, testing him with all her hundred and one coquetries, not infrequently thought to detect a spark of response.

Joaz Banbeck dismounted from the Spider, ordered

9

it back to its quarters. Phade came diffidently forward, and Joaz turned her a quizzical look. "What requires so urgent a summons? Have you remembered the nineteenth location?"

Phade flushed in confusion. Artlessly she had described the painstaking rigors of her training; Joaz now referred to an item in one of the classifications which had slipped her mind.

Phade spoke rapidly, excited once more. "I opened the door into your study, softly, gently. And what did I see? A sacerdote, naked in his hair! He did not hear me. I shut the door, I ran to fetch Rife. When we returned—the chamber was empty!"

Joaz's eyebrows contracted a trifle; he looked up the valley. "Odd." After a moment he asked, "You are sure that he saw nothing of you?"

"No. I think not. Yet, when I returned with stupid old Rife he had disappeared! Is it true that they know magic?"

"As to that, I cannot say," replied Joaz.

They returned up Kergan's Way, traversed tunnels and rock-walled corridors, finally came to the entry chamber. Rife once more dozed at his desk. Joaz signaled Phade back, and going quietly forward, thrust aside the door to his study. He glanced here and there, nostrils twitching. The room was empty. He climbed the stairs, investigated the sleeping parlor, returned to the study. Unless magic were indeed involved, the sacerdote had provided himself a secret entrance. With this thought in mind, he swung back the bookcase door, descended to the workshop, and again tested the air for the sour-sweet odor of the sacerdotes. A trace? Possibly.

Joaz examined the room inch by inch, peering from every angle. At last, along the wall below the bench, he discovered a barely perceptible crack, marking out an oblong.

Joaz nodded with dour satisfaction. He rose to his feet, returned to his study. He considered his shelves. What was here to interest a sacerdote? Books, folios, pamphlets? Had they even mastered the art of reading? When next I meet a sacerdote I must inquire, thought Joaz vaguely; at least he will tell me the truth. On second thought, he knew the question to be ludicrous; the sacerdotes, for all their nakedness, were by no means barbarians, and in fact had provided him his four vision-panes—a feat of no small skill.

He inspected the yellowed marble glove which he considered his most valued possession—a representation of mythical Eden. Apparently it had not been disturbed. Another shelf displayed models of the Banbeck dragons—the rust-red Termagant; the Long-horned Murderer and its cousin the Striding Murderer; the Blue Horror; the Fiend, low to the ground, immensely strong, tail tipped with a steel barbel; the ponderous Jugger, skull-cap polished and white as an egg.

A little apart stood the progenitor of the entire group—a pearl-pallid creature upright on two legs, with two versatile central members, a pair of multi-articulated brachs at the neck. Beautifully detailed though these models might be, why should they pique the curiosity of a sacerdote? No reason whatever, when the originals could be studied daily without hindrance.

What of the workshop, then? Joaz rubbed his long pale chin. He had no illusions about the value of his work. Idle tinkering, no more. Joaz put aside conjecture. Most likely the sacerdote had come upon no specific mission, the visit perhaps being part of a continued inspection. But why?

A pounding at the door: old Rife's irreverent fist. Joaz opened to him.

"Joaz Banbeck, a notice from Ervis Carcolo of Happy Valley. He wishes to confer with you, and at this moment awaits your response on Banbeck Verge."

"Very well," said Joaz. "I will confer with Ervis Carcolo."

"Here? Or on Banbeck Verge?"

"On the Verge, in half an hour."

CHAPTER 2

TEN MILES from Banbeck Vale, across a wind-scoured wilderness of ridges, crags, spines of stone, amazing crevasses, barren fells and fields of tumbled boulders lay Happy Valley. As wide as Banbeck Vale but only half as long and half as deep, its bed of wind-deposited soil was only half as thick and correspondingly less productive.

The chief councilor of Happy Valley was Ervis Carcolo, a thick-bodied, short-legged man with a vehement face, a heavy mouth, a disposition by turns jocose and wrathful. Unlike Joaz Banbeck, Carcolo enjoyed nothing more than his visits to the dragon barracks, where he treated dragon masters, grooms and dragons alike to a spate of bawled criticism, exhortation, invective.

Ervis Carcolo was an energetic man, intent upon restoring Happy Valley to the ascendancy it had enjoyed some twelve generations before. During these harsh times, before the advent of the dragons, men fought their own battles, and the men of Happy Valley had been notably daring, deft and ruthless. Banbeck Vale, the Great Northern Rift, Clewhaven, Sadro Valley, and Phosphor Gulch all acknowledged the authority of the Carcolos.

Then down from space came a ship of the Basics, or grephs, as they were known at that time. The ship killed or took prisoner the entire population of Clewhaven; attempted as much in the Great Northern Rift, but only partially succeeded; then bombarded the remaining settlements with explosive pellets. When the survivors crept back to their devastated valleys, the dominance of Happy Valley was a fiction. A generation later, during the Age of Wet Iron, even the fiction collapsed. In a climactic battle Goss Carcolo was captured by Kergan Banbeck and forced to emasculate himself with his own knife.

13

Five years of peace elapsed, and then the Basics returned. After depopulating Sadro Valley, the great black ship landed in Banbeck Vale, but the inhabitants had taken warning and had fled into the mountains. Toward nightfall twenty-three of the Basics sallied forth behind their precisely trained warriors. There were several platoons of Heavy Troops, a squad of Weaponeers—these hardly distinguishable from the men of Aerlith—and a squad of Trackers. These later were emphatically different. The sunset storm broke over the Vale, rendering the fliers from the ship useless, which allowed Kergan Banbeck to perform the amazing feat which made his name a legend on Aerlith. Rather than joining the terrified flight of his people to the High Jambles, he assembled sixty warriors, shamed them to courage with jeers and taunts. Leaping from ambush they hacked to pieces one platoon of the Heavy Troops, routed the others, captured the twenty-three Basics almost before they realized that anything was amiss. The Weaponeers stood back frantic with frustration, unable to use their weapons for fear of destroying their masters. The Heavy Troopers blundered forward to attack, halting only when Kergan Banbeck would be the first to die. Confused, the Heavy Troopers drew back; Kergan Banbeck, his men and the twenty-three captives escaped into the darkness.

The long Aerlith night passed; the dawn storm swept out of the east, thundered overhead, retreated majestically into the west; Skene rose like a blazing storm. Three men emerged from the Basic ship—a Weaponeer and a pair of Trackers. They climbed the cliffs to Banbeck Verge, while above flitted a small Basic flier, no more than a buoyant platform, diving and veering in the wind like a poorly-balanced kite. The three men trudged south toward the High Jambles, a region of chaotic shadows and lights, splintered rock and fallen crags, boulders heaped on boulders. It was the traditional refuge of hunted men.

Halting in front of the Jambles the Weaponeer called out for Kergan Banbeck, asking him to parley.

Kergan Banbeck came forth, and now ensued the strangest colloquy in the history of Aerlith. The Weaponeer spoke the language of men with difficulty, his lips, tongue and glottal passages more adapted to the language of the Basics.

"You are restraining twenty-three of our Revered. It is necessary that you usher them forth, in all humility." He spoke soberly, with an air of gentle melancholy, neither asserting, commanding, nor urging. As his linguistic habits had been shaped to Basic patterns, so with his mental processes.

Kergan Banbeck, a tall spare man with varnished black eyebrows, black hair shaped and varnished into a crest of five tall spikes, gave a bark of humorless laughter. "What of the Aerlith folk killed? What of the folk seized aboard your ship?"

The Weaponeer bent forward earnestly, himself an impressive man with a noble aquiline head. He was hairless except for small rolls of wispy yellow fleece.

His skin shone as if burnished; his ears, where he differed most noticeably from the unadapted men of Aerlith, were small fragile flaps.

He wore a simple garment of dark blue and white, carried no weapons save a small multi-purpose ejector. With complete poise and quiet reasonableness he responded to Kergan Banbeck's questions. "The Aerlith folk who have been killed are dead. Those aboard the ship will be merged into the understratum, where the infusion of fresh outside blood is of value."

Kergan Banbeck inspected the Weaponeer with contemptuous deliberation. In some respects, thought Kergan Banbeck, this modified and carefully inbred man resembled the sacerdotes of his own planet, notably in the clear fair skin, the strongly modeled features, the long legs and arms. Perhaps telepathy was at work, or perhaps a trace of the characteristic soursweet odor had been carried to him. Turning his head he noticed a sacerdote standing among the rocks not fifty feet away—a man naked except for his golden torc and long brown hair blowing behind him like a pennant. By the ancient etiquette, Kergan Banbeck looked through him, pretended that he had no existence. The Weaponeer after a swift glance did likewise.

"I demand that you release the folk of Aerlith from your ship," said Kergan Banbeck in a flat voice.

The Weaponeer smilingly shook his head, bent his best efforts to the task of making himself intelligible. "These persons are not under discussion; their—" he paused, seeking words, "—their destiny is . . . parceled, quantum-type, ordained. Established. Nothing can be said more."

Kergan Banbeck's smile became a cynical grimace. He stood aloof and silent while the Weaponeer croaked on. The sacerdote came slowly forward, a few steps at a time. "You will understand," said the Weaponeer, "that a pattern for events exists. It is the function of such as myself to shape events so that they will fit the pattern." He bent, with a graceful sweep of arm seized a small jagged pebble. "Just as I can grind this bit of rock to fit a round aperture."

Kergan Banbeck reached forward, took the pebble, tossed it high over the tumbled boulders. "That bit of rock you shall never shape to fit a round hole."

The Weaponeer shook his head in mild deprecation. "There is always more rock."

"And there are always more holes," declared Kergan Banbeck.

"To business then," said the Weaponeer. "I propose to shape this situation to its correct arrangement."

"What do you offer in exchange for the twenty-three grephs?"

The Weaponeer gave his shoulder an uneasy shake. The ideas of this man were as wild, barbaric and arbitrary as the varnished spikes of his hairdress. "If you desire I will give you instruction and advice, so that—"

Kergan Banbeck made a sudden gesture. "I make three conditions." The sacerdote now stood only ten feet away, face blind, gaze vague. "First," said Ker-

17

gan Banbeck, "a guarantee against future attacks upon the men of Aerlith. Five grephs must always remain in our custody as hostages. Secondly—further to secure the perpetual validity of the guarantee—you must deliver me a spaceship, equipped, energized, armed, and you must instruct me in its use."

The Weaponeer threw back his head, made a series of bleating sounds through his nose. "Thirdly," continued Kergan Banbeck, "you must release all the men and women presently aboard your ship."

The Weaponeer blinked, spoke rapid hoarse words of amazement to the Trackers. They stirred, uneasy and impatient, watching Kergan Banbeck sidelong as if he were not only savage, but mad. Overhead hovered the flier; the Weaponeer looked up and seemed to derive encouragement from the sight. Turning back to Kergan Banbeck was a firm fresh attitude, he spoke as if the previous interchange had never occurred. "I have come to instruct you that the twenty-three Revered must be instantly released."

Kergan Banbeck repeated his own demands. "You must furnish me a spaceship, you must raid no more, you must release the captives. Do you agree, yes or no?"

The Weaponeer seemed confused. "This is a peculiar situation—indefinite, unquantizable."

"Can you not understand me?" barked Kergan Banbeck in exasperation. He glanced at the sacerdote, an act of questionable decorum, then performed in manner completely unconventional. "Sacerdote, how can I deal with this blockhead? He does not seem to hear me."

The sacerdote moved a step nearer, his face as bland and blank as before. Living by a doctrine which proscribed active or intentional interference in the affairs of other men, he could make to any question only a specific and limited answer. "He hears you, but there is no meeting of ideas between you. His thought-structure is derived from that of his masters, and is incommensurable with yours. As to how you must deal with him, I cannot say."

Kergan Banbeck looked back to the Weaponeer. "Have you heard what I asked of you? Did you understand my conditions for the release of the grephs?"

"I heard you distinctly," replied the Weaponeer. "Your words have no meaning, they are absurdities, paradoxes. Listen to me carefully. It is ordained, complete, a quantum of destiny, that you deliver to us the Revered. It is irregular, it is not ordainment that you should have a ship, or that your other demands be met."

Kergan Banbeck's face became red; he half-turned toward his men, but restraining his anger, spoke slowly and with careful clarity. "I have something you want. You have something I want. Let us trade."

For twenty seconds the two men stared eye to eye. Then the Weaponeer drew a deep breath. "I will explain in your words, so that you will comprehend. Certainties—no, not certainties; definites—definites exist. These are units of certainty, quanta of necessity and order. Existence is the steady succession of these units, one after the other. The activity of the universe can be expressed by reference to those units. Irregularity, absurdity—these are like half a man, with half a brain, half a heart, half of all his vital organs. Neither are allowed to exist. That you hold twenty-three Revered as captives is such an absurdity, an outrage to the rational flow of the universe."

Kergan Banbeck threw up his hands, turned once more to the sacerdote. "How can I halt his nonsense? How can I make him see reason?"

The sacerdote reflected. "He speaks not nonsense, but rather a language you fail to understand. You can make him understand your language by erasing all knowledge and training from his mind, and replacing it with patterns of your own."

Kergan Banbeck fought back an unsettling sense of frustration and unreality. In order to elicit exact answers from a sacerdote, an exact question was required; indeed it was remarkable that this sacerdote stayed to be questioned. Thinking carefully, he asked, "How do you suggest that I deal with this man?"

"Release the twenty-three grephs." The sacerdote touched the twin knobs at the front of his golden torc: a ritual gesture indicating that, no matter how reluctantly, he had performed an act which conceivably might alter the course of the future. Again he tapped his torc, and intoned, "Release the grephs; he will then depart."

Kergan Banbeck cried out in unrestrained anger.

"Who then do you serve? Man or greph? Let us have the truth! Speak!"

"By my faith, by my creed, by the truth of my *tand* I serve no one by myself." The sacerdote turned his face toward the great crag of Mount Gethron and moved slowly off; the wind blew his long fine hair to the side.

Kergan Banbeck watched him go, then with cold decisiveness turned back to the Weaponeer. "Your discussion of certainties and absurdities is interesting. I feel that you have confused the two. Here is certainty from my viewpoint! I will not release the twenty-three grephs unless you meet my terms. If you attack us further, I will cut them in half, to illustrate and realize your figure of speech, and perhaps convince you that absurdities are possible. I say no more."

The Weaponeer shook his head slowly, pityingly. "Listen, I will explain. Certain conditions are unthinkable, they are unquantized, undestined—"

"Go," thundered Kergan Banbeck. "Otherwise you will join your twenty-three revered grephs, and I will teach you how real the unthinkable can become!"

The Weaponeer and the two Trackers, croaking and muttering, turned, retreated from the Jambles to Banbeck Verge, descended into the valley. Over them the flier darted, veered, fluttered, settled like a falling leaf.

Watching their retreat among the crags the men of

21

Banbeck Vale presently witnessed a remarkable scene. Half an hour after the Weaponeer had returned to the ship, he came leaping forth once again, dancing, cavorting. Others followed him—Weaponeers, Trackers, Heavy Troopers and eight more grephs—all jerking, jumping, running back and forth in distracted steps. The ports of the ship flashed lights of various colors, and there came a slow sound of tortured machinery.

"They have gone mad!" muttered Kergan Banbeck. He hesitated an instant, then gave an order. "Assemble every man; we attack while they are helpless!"

Down from the High Jambles rushed the men of Banbeck Vale. As they descended the cliffs, a few of the captured men and women from Sadro Valley came timidly forth from the ship and meeting no restraint fled to freedom across Banbeck Vale. Others followed—and now the Banbeck warriors reached the valley floor.

Beside the ship the insanity had quieted; the outworlders huddled quietly beside the hull. There came a sudden mind-shattering explosion; a blankness of yellow and white fire. The ship disintegrated. A great crater marred the valley floor; fragments of metal began to fall among the attacking Banbeck warriors.

Kergan Banbeck stared at the scene of destruction. Slowly, his shoulders sagging, he summoned his people and led them back to their ruined valley. At the rear, marching single-file, tied together with ropes, came the twenty-three grephs, dull-eyed, pliant, already remote from their previous existence. The texture of Destiny was inevitable: the present circumstances could not apply to twenty-three of the Revered. The mechanism must therefore adjust to insure the halcyon progression of events. The twenty-three, hence, were something other than the Revered: a different order of creature entirely. If this were true, what were they? Asking each other the question in sad croaking undertones, they marched down the cliff into Banbeck Vale.

CHAPTER 3

ACROSS THE LONG Aerlith years the fortunes of Happy Valley and Banbeck Vale fluctuated with the capabilities of the opposing Carcolos and Banbecks. Golden Banbeck, Joaz's grandfather, was forced to release Happy Valley from clientship when Uttern Carcolo, an accomplished dragon-breeder, produced the first Fiends. Golden Banbeck, in his turn, developed the Juggers, but allowed an uneasy truce to continue.

Further years passed; Ilden Banbeck, the son of Golden, a frail ineffectual man, was killed in a fall from a mutinous Spider. With Joaz yet an ailing child, Grode Carcolo decided to try his chances against Banbeck Vale. He failed to reckon with old Hendel Banbeck, grand-uncle to Joaz and Chief Dragon Master. The Happy Valley forces were routed on Starbreak

Fell; Grode Carcolo was killed and young Ervis gored by a Murderer. For various reasons, including Hendel's age and Joaz's youth, the Banbeck army failed to press to a decisive advantage. Ervis Carcolo, though exhausted by loss of blood and pain, withdrew in some degree of order, and for further years a suspicious truce held between the neighboring valleys.

Joaz matured into a saturnine young man, who, if he excited no enthusiastic affection from his people, at least aroused no violent dislike. He and Ervis Carcolo were united in a mutual contempt. At the mention of Joaz's study, with its books, scrolls, models and plans, its complicated viewing-system across Banbeck Vale (the optics furnished, it was rumored, by the sacerdotes), Carcolo would throw up his hands in disgust. "Learning? Pah! What avails all this rolling in bygone vomit? Where does it lead? He should have been born a sacerdote; he is the same sort of sour-mouthed cloudminded weakling!"

An intinerant, one Dae Alvonso, who combined the trades of minstrel, child-buyer, psychiatrist and chiropractor, reported Carcolo's obloquies to Joaz, who shrugged. "Ervis Carcolo should breed himself to one of his own Juggers," said Joaz. "He would thereby produce an impregnable creature with the Jugger's armor and his own unflinching stupidity."

The remark in due course returned to Ervis Carcolo, and by coincidence, touched him in a particularly sore spot. Secretly he had been attempting an innovation at his brooders: a dragon almost as mas-

24

sive as the Jugger with the savage intelligence and agility of the Blue Horror. But Ervis Carcolo worked with an intuitive and over-optimistic approach, ignoring the advice of Bast Givven, his Chief Dragon Master.

The eggs hatched; a dozen spratlings survived. Ervis Carcolo nurtured them with alternate tenderness and objurgation. Eventually the dragons matured. Carcolo's hoped for combination of fury and impregnability was realized in four sluggish irritable creatures, with bloated torsos, spindly legs, insatiable appetites. ("As if one can breed a dragon by commanding it: 'Exist!'" sneered Bast Givven to his helpers, and advised them, "Be wary of the beasts; they are competent only at luring you within reach of their brachs.")

The time, effort, facilities, and provender wasted upon the useless hybrid had weakened Carcolo's army. Of the fecund Termagants he had no lack; there was a sufficiency of Long-horned Murderers and Striding Monsters, but the heavier and more specialized types, especially Juggers, were far from adequate to his plans. The memory of Happy Valley's ancient glory haunted his dreams; first he would subdue Banbeck Vale, and often he planned the ceremony whereby he would reduce Joaz Banbeck to the office of apprentice barracks boy.

Ervis Carcolo's ambitions were complicated by a set of basic difficulties. Happy Valley's population had doubled, but rather than extending the city by breaching new pinnacles or driving tunnels, Carcolo constructed three new dragon-brooders, a dozen barracks and an enormous training compound. The folk of the valley could choose either to cram the fetid existing tunnels or build ramshackle dwellings along the base of the cliff. Brooders, barracks, training fields; water was diverted from the pond to maintain the brooders; enormous quantities of produce went to feed dragons. The folk of Happy Valley, undernourished, sickly, miserable, shared none of Carcolo's aspirations, and their lack of enthusiasm infuriated him.

In any event, when the itinerant Dae Alvonso repeated Joaz Banbeck's recommendation that Ervis Carcolo breed himself to a Jugger, Carcolo seethed with choler. "Bah!" What does Joaz Banbeck know about dragon-breeding? I doubt if he understands his own dragon-talk." He referred to the means by which orders and instructions were transmitted to the dragons: a secret jargon distinctive to every army. To learn an opponent's dragon-talk was the prime goal of every Dragon Master, for he thereby gained a certain degree of control over his enemies' forces. "I am a practical man, worth two of him," Carcolo went on. "Can he design, nurture, rear and teach dragons? Can he impose discipline, teach ferocity? No. He leaves all this to his dragon masters, while he lolls on a couch eating sweetmeats, campaigning only against the patience of his minstrel-maidens. They say that by astrological divination he predicts the return of the Basics, that he walks with his neck cocked, watching the sky. Is such a man deserving of power and a prosperous life? I say no. Is Ervis Carcolo of Happy Valley such a man? I say yes, and this I will demonstrate."

Dae Alvonso judiciously held up his hand. "Not so fast. He is more alert than you think. His dragons are in prime condition; he visits them often. And as for the Basics—"

"Do not speak to me of Basics," stormed Carcolo. "I am no child to be frightened by bugbears!"

Again Dae Alvonso held up his hand. "Listen. I am serious, and you can profit by my news. Joaz Banbeck took me into his study—"

"The famous study, indeed!"

"From a cabinet he brought out a ball of crystal mounted on a black box."

"Aha!" jeered Carcolo. "A crystal ball!"

Dae Alvonso went on placidly, ignoring the interruption. "I examined this globe, and indeed it seemed to hold all of space; within it floated stars and planets, all the bodies of the cluster. 'Look well,' said Joaz Banbeck, 'you will never see the like of this anywhere. It was built by the olden men and brought to Aerlith when our people first arrived.'

" 'Indeed,' I said. 'And what is this object?'

" 'It is a celestial armamentarium,' said Joaz. 'It depicts all the nearby stars, and their positions at any time I choose to specify. Now,' here he pointed, 'see this white dot? This is our sun. See this red star? In the old alamanacs it is named Coralyne. It swings

27

near us at irregular intervals, for such is the flow of stars in this cluster. These intervals have always co-incided with the attacks of the Basics.'

"Here I expressed astonishment; Joaz assured me regarding the matter. The history of men on Aerlith records six attacks by the Basics, or grephs as they were originally known. Apparently as Coralyne swings through space the Basics scour nearby worlds for hidden dens of humanity. The last of these was long ago during the time of Kergan Banbeck, with the results you know about. At that time Coralyne passed close in the heavens. For the first time since, Coralyne is once more close at hand.' This," Alvonso told Carcolo, "is what Joaz Banbeck told me, and this is what I saw."

Carcolo was impressed in spite of himself. "Do you mean to tell me," demanded Carcolo, "that within this globe swim all the stars of space?"

"As to that, I cannot vouch," replied Dae Alvonso. "The globe is set in a black box, and I suspect that an inner mechanism projects images or perhaps con-trols luminous spots which stimulate the stars. Either way it is a marvelous device, one which I would be proud to own. I offered Joaz several precious objects in exchange, but he would have none of them."

Carcolo curled his lip in disgust. "You and your stolen children. Have you no shame?"

"No more than my customers," said Dae Alvonso stoutly. "As I recall, I have dealt profitably with you on several occasions."

Ervis Carcolo turned away, pretended to watch a pair of Termagants exercising with wooden scimitars. The two men stood by a stone fence behind which scores of dragons practiced evolutions, duel with spears, swords, strengthened muscles. Scales flashed, dust rose up under splayed stamping feet; the acrid odor of dragon-sweat permeated the air.

Carcolo muttered, "He is crafty, that Joaz. He knew you would report to me in detail."

Dae Alvonso nodded. "Precisely. His words were— but perhaps I should be discreet." He glanced slyly toward Carcolo from under shaggy white eyebrows.

"Speak," said Ervis Carcolo gruffly.

"Very well. Mind you, I quote Joaz Banbeck. 'Tell blundering old Carcolo that he is in great danger. If the Basics return to Aerlith, as well they may, Happy Valley is absolutely vulnerable and will be ruined. Where can his people hide? They will be herded into the black ship, transported to a cold new planet. If Carcolo is not completely heartless he will drive new tunnels, prepare hidden avenues. Otherwise—'"

"Otherwise what?" demanded Carcolo.

" 'Otherwise there will be no more Happy Valley, no more Ervis Carcolo.' "

"Bah," said Carcolo in a subdued voice. "The young jackanapes barks in shrill tones."

"Perhaps he extends an honest warning. His further words . . . But I fear to offend your dignity."

"Continue! Speak!"

"These are his words—but no, I dare not repeat

29

them. Essentially he considers your efforts to create an army ludicrous; he contrasts your intelligence unfavorably to his own; he predicts—"

"Enough!" roared Ervis Carcolo, waving his fists. "He is a subtle adversary, but why do you lend yourself to his tricks?"

Dae Alvonso shook his frosty old head. "I merely repeat, with reluctance, that which you demand to hear. Now then, since you have wrung me dry, do me some profit. Will you buy drugs, elixirs, wambles, or potions? I have here a salve of eternal youth while I stole from the Demie Sacerdote's personal coffer. In my train are both boy and girl children, obsequious and handsome, at a fair price. I will listen to your woes, cure your lisp, guarantee a placidity of disposition—or perhaps you would buy dragon eggs?"

"I need none of those," grunted Carcolo. "Especially dragon's eggs which hatch to lizards. As for children, Happy Valley seethes with them. Bring me a dozen sound Juggers, you may depart with a hundred children of your choice."

Dae Alvonso shook his head sadly, lurched away. Carcolo slumped against the fence, staring across the dragon pens.

The sun hung low over the crags of Mount Despoire; evening was close at hand. This was the most pleasant time of the Aerlith day, when the winds ceased, leaving a vast velvet quiet. Skene's blaze softened to a smoky yellow, with a bronze aureole; the clouds of the approaching evening storm gathered, rose, fell, shifted, swirled, glowing and changing in

30

every tone of gold, orange-brown, gold-brown and dusty violet.

Skene sank; the golds and oranges became oak-brown and purple; lightning threaded the clouds and the rain fell in a black curtain. In the barracks men moved with vigilance, for now the dragons became unpredictable—by turns watchful, torpid, quarrelsome. With the passing of the rain, evening became night, and a cool quiet breeze drifted through the valleys. The dark sky began to burn and dazzle with the stars of the cluster. One of the most effulgent twinkled red, green, white, red, green.

Ervis Carcolo studied this star thoughtfully. One idea led to another, and presently to a course of action which seemed to dissolve the entire tangle of uncertainties and dissatisfactions which marred his life. Carcolo twisted his mouth to a sour grimace; he must make overtures to that popinjay Joaz Banbeck —but if this were unavoidable: so be it!

Hence, the following morning, shortly after Phade the minstrel-maiden discovered the sacerdote in Joaz's study, a messenger appeared in the Vale, inviting Joaz Banbeck up to Banbeck Verge for a conference with Ervis Carcolo.

CHAPTER 4

ERVIS CARCOLO waited on Banbeck Verge with Chief Dragon Master Bast Givven and a pair of young fuglemen. Behind, in a row, stood their mounts: four glistening Spiders, brachs folded, legs splayed at exactly identical angles. These were of Carcolo's newest breed, and he was immoderately proud of them. The barbs surrounding the horny visages were clasped with cinnabar cabochons; a round target enameled black and studded with a central spike covered each chest. The men wore the traditional black leather breeches, with short maroon cloaks, black leather helmets, with long flaps slanting back across the ears and down to the shoulders.

The four men waited, patient or restless as their natures dictated, surveying the well-tended length of Banbeck Vale. To the south stretched fields of various food stuffs: vetch, bellegarde, moss-cake, a loquat grove. Directly opposite, near the mouth of Clybourne Crevasse the shape of the crater created by the explosion of the Basic ship could still be seen. North lay more fields, then the dragon compounds, consisting of black-brick barracks, a brooder, an exercise field. Beyond lay Banbeck Jambles, an area of wasteland, where ages previously a section of the cliff had fallen, creating a wilderness of tumbled rock, similar to the High Jambles under Mount Gethron, but smaller in compass.

One of the young fuglemen rather tactlessly commented upon the evident prosperity of Banbeck Vale, to the implicit deprecation of Happy Valley. Ervis Carcolo listened glumly a moment or two, then turned a haughty stare toward the offender.

"Notice the dam," said the fugleman. "We waste half our water in seepage."

"True," said the other. "That rock facing is a good idea. I wonder why we don't do something similar."

Carcolo started to speak, thought better of it. With a growling sound in his throat, he turned away. Bast Givven made a sign; the fuglemen fell silent.

A few moments later Givven announced; "Joaz Banbeck has set forth."

Carcolo peered down toward Kergan's Way. "Where is his company? Does he ride alone?"

"So it seems."

A few minutes later Joaz Banbeck appeared on Banbeck Verge riding a Spider caparisoned in gray and red velvet. Joaz wore a loose lounge cloak of soft brown cloth over a gray shirt and gray trousers, with a long-billed hat of blue velvet. He held up his hand in casual greeting; brusquely Ervis Carcolo returned the salute, and with a jerk of his head sent Givven and the fuglemen off out of earshot.

Carcolo said gruffly, "You sent me a message by old Alvonso."

Joaz nodded. "I trust he rendered my remarks accurately?"

Carcolo grinned wolfishly. "At times he felt obliged to paraphrase."

"Tactful old Dae Alvonso."

"I am given to understand," said Carcolo, "that you consider me rash, ineffectual, callous to the best interests of Happy Valley, Alvonso admitted that you used the word 'blunderer' in reference to me."

33

Joaz smiled politely. "Sentiments of this sort are best transmitted through intermediaries."

Carcolo made a great show of dignified forbearance. "Apparently you feel that another Basic attack is imminent."

"Just so," agreed Joaz, "if my theory, which puts their home at the star Coralyne, is correct. In which case, as I pointed out to Alvonso, Happy Valley is seriously vulnerable."

"And why not Banbeck Vale as well?" barked Carcolo.

Joaz stared at him in surprise. "Is it not obvious? I have taken precautions. My people are housed in tunnels, rather than huts. We have several escape routes, should this prove necessary, both to High Jambles and to Banbeck Jambles."

"Very interesting." Carcolo made an effort to soften his voice. "If your theory is accurate—and I pass no immediate judgment—then perhaps I would be wise to take similar measures. But I think in different terms. I prefer attack, activity, to passive defense."

"Admirable," said Joaz Banbeck. "Important deeds are done by men such as you."

Carcolo became a trifle pink in the face. "This is neither here nor there," he said. "I have come to propose a joint project. It is entirely novel, but carefully thought out. I have considered various aspects of this matter for several years."

"I attend you with great interest," said Joaz.

Carcolo blew out his cheeks. "You know the legends as well as I, perhaps better. Our people came

34

to Aerlith as exiles during the War of the Ten Stars. The Nightmare Coalition apparently had defeated the Old Rule, but how the war ended—" he threw up his hands, "who can say?"

"There is a significant indication," said Joaz. "The Basics revisit Aerlith and ravage us at their pleasure. We have seen no men, except those who serve the Basics."

"'Men?'" Carcolo demanded scornfully. "I call them something else. Nevertheless, this is no more than a deduction, and we are ignorant as to the course of history. Perhaps Basics rule the cluster, perhaps they plague us only because we are weak and weaponless. Perhaps we are the last men; perhaps the Old Rule is resurgent. And never forget that many years have elapsed since the Basics last appeared on Aerlith."

"Many years have elapsed since Aerlith and Coralyne were in such convenient apposition."

Carcolo made an impatient gesture. "A supposition, which may or may not be relevant. Let me explain the basic axiom of my proposal. It is simple enough. I feel that Banbeck Vale and Happy Valley are too small a compass for men such as ourselves. We deserve larger scope."

Joaz agreed. "I wish it were possible to ignore the practical difficulties involved."

"I am able to suggest a method to counter these difficulties," asserted Carcolo.

"In that case," said Joaz, "power, glory and wealth are as good as ours."

Carcolo glanced at him sharply, slapped his breeches with the gold-beaded tassel to his scabbard. "Reflect," he said. "The sacerdotes inhabited Aerlith before us. How long no one can say. It is a mystery. In fact, what do we know of the sacerdotes? Next to nothing. They trade their metal and glass for our food, they live in deep caverns, their creed is disassociation, reverie, detachment, whatever one may wish to call it—totally incomprehensible to one such as myself." He challenged Joaz with a look; Joaz merely fingered his long chin. "They put themselves forward as simple metaphysical cultists; actually they are a very mysterious people. Has anyone yet seen a sacerdote woman? What of the blue lights, what of the lightning towers, what of the sacerdote magic? What of weird comings and goings by night, what of strange shapes moving across the sky, perhaps to other planets?"

"The tales exist, certainly," said Joaz. "As to the degree of credence to be placed in them—"

"Now we reach the meat of my proposal!" declared Ervis Carcolo. "The creed of the sacerdotes apparently forbids shame, inhibition, fear, regard for consequence. Hence, they are forced to answer any question put to them. Nevertheless, creed or no creed, they completely befog any information an assiduous man is able to wheedle from them."

Joaz inspected him curiously. "Evidently you have made the attempt."

Ervis Carcolo nodded. "Yes. Why should I deny it? I have questioned three sacerdotes with determination and persistence. They answered all my questions with gravity and calm reflection, but told me nothing." He shook his head in vexation. "Therefore, I suggest that we apply coercion."

"You are a brave man."

Carcolo shook his head modestly. "I would dare no direct measures. But they must eat. If Banbeck Vale and Happy Valley co-operate, we can apply a very cogent persuasion: hunger. Presently their words may be more to the point."

Joaz considered a moment or two. Ervis Carcolo twitched his scabbard tassel. "Your plan," said Joaz at last, "is not a frivolous one, and is ingenious—at least, at first glance. What sort of information do you hope to secure? In short, what are your ultimate aims?"

Carcolo sidled close, prodded Joaz with his fore-finger. "We know nothing of the outer worlds. We are marooned on this miserable world of stone and wind while life passes us by. You assume that Basics rule the cluster, but suppose you are wrong? Suppose the Old Rule has returned? Think of the rich cities, the gay resorts, the palaces, the pleasure islands! Look up into the night sky, ponder the bounties which might be ours! You ask how can we implement these desires? I respond, the process may be so simple that the sacerdotes will reveal it without reluctance."

"You mean—"

"Communication with the worlds of men! Deliverance from this lonely little world at the edge of the universe!"

Joaz Banbeck nodded dubiously. "A fine vision, but the evidence suggests a situation far different, namely the destruction of man, and the Human Empire."

Carcolo held out his hands in a gesture of open-minded tolerance. "Perhaps you are right. But why should we not make inquiries of the sacerdotes? Concretely I propose as follows. First, that you and I agree to the mutual cause I have outlined. Next, we request an audience with Demie Sacerdote. We put our questions. If he responds freely, well and good. If he evades, then we act in mutuality. No more food to the sacerdotes until they inform us clearly and frankly what we want to hear."

"Other valleys, vales, and gulches exist," said Joaz thoughtfully.

Carcolo made a brisk gesture. "We can deter any such trade by persuasion or by the power of our dragons."

"The essence of your idea appeals to me," said Joaz, "but I fear that all is not so simple."

Carcolo rapped his thigh smartly with the tassel. "And why not?"

"In the first place, Coralyne shines bright in the sky. This is our first concern. Should Coralyne pass, should the Basics not attack—then is the time to pursue this matter. Again—and perhaps more to the point—I doubt that we can starve the sacerdotes into submission. In fact, I think it highly unlikely. I will go farther. I consider it impossible."

Carcolo blinked. "In what wise?"

"They walk naked through sleet and storm; do you

think they fear hunger? And there is wild lichen to be gathered. How could we forbid this? You might dare some sort of coercion, but not I. The tales told of the sacerdotes may be no more than superstition —or they may be understatement."

Ervis Carcolo heaved a deep disgusted sigh. "Joaz Banbeck, I took you for a man of decision. But you merely pick flaws."

"These are not flaws, they are major errors which would lead to disaster."

"Well, then, do you have any suggestions of your own?"

Joaz fingered his chin. "If Coralyne recedes and we are still on Aerlith—rather than in the hold of the Basic ship—then let us plan to plunder the secrets of the sacerdotes. In the meantime I strongly recommend that you prepare Happy Valley against a new raid. You are over-extended, with your new brooders and barracks. Let them rest, while you dig yourself secure tunnels!"

Ervis Carcolo stared straight across Banbeck Vale. "I am not a man to defend. I attack!"

"You will attack heat beams and ion rays with your dragons?"

Ervis Carcolo turned his gaze back to Joaz Banbeck. "Can I consider us allies in the plan I have proposed?"

"In its broadest principles, certainly. However, I don't care to co-operate in starving or otherwise coercing the sacerdotes. It might be dangerous, as well as futile."

For an instant Carcolo could not control his detestation of Joaz Banbeck; his lip curled, his hands clenched. "Danger! Bah! What danger from a handful of naked pacifists?"

"We do not know that they are pacifists. We do know that they are men."

Carcolo once more became brightly cordial. "Perhaps you are right. But—essentially at least—we are allies."

"To a degree."

"Good. I suggest that in the case of the attack you fear, we act together, with a common strategy."

Joaz nodded distantly. "This might be effective."

"Let us co-ordinate our plans. Let us assume that the Basics drop down into Banbeck Vale. I suggest that your folk take refuge in Happy Valley, while the Happy Valley army joins with yours to cover their retreat. And likewise, should they attack Happy Valley, my people will take refuge in Banbeck Vale."

Joaz laughed in sheer amusement. "Ervis Carcolo, what sort of lunatic do you take me for? Return to your valley, put aside your foolish grandiosities, dig yourself protection. And fast! Coralyne is bright!"

Carcolo stood stiffly. "Do I understand that you reject my offer of alliance?"

"Not at all. But I cannot undertake to protect you and your people if you will not help yourselves. Meet my requirements, satisfy me that you are a fit ally— then we shall speak further."

Ervis Carcolo whirled on his heel, signaled to Bast Givven and the two young fuglemen. With no further word or glance he mounted his splendid Spider, goaded him into a sudden leaping run across the Verge, and up the slope toward Starbreak Fell. His men followed, less precipitously.

Joaz watched him go, shaking his head in sad wonder. Then mounting his own Spider he returned down the trail to the floor of Banbeck Vale.

CHAPTER 5

THE LONG Aerlith day, equivalent to six of the old Diurnal Units, passed. In Happy Valley there was grim activity, a sense of purpose and impending decision. The dragons exercised in tighter formation, the fuglemen and cornets called orders with harsher voices. In the armory bullets were cast, powder mixed, swords ground and honed.

Ervis Carcolo drove himself with dramatic bravado, wearing out Spider after Spider as he sent his dragons through various evolutions. In the case of the Happy Valley forces, these were for the most part Termagants—small active dragons with rust-red scales, narrow darting heads, chisel-sharp fangs. Their brachs were strong and well developed: they used lance, cutlass or mace with equal skill. A man pitted against a Termagant stood no chance, for the scales warded off bullets as well as any blow the man might have strength enough to deal. On the other hand a single slash of fang, the rip of a scythe-like claw, meant death to the man.

The Termagants were fecund and hardy and throve even under the conditions which existed in the Happy Valley brooders; hence their predominance in Carcolo's army. This was a situation not to the liking of Bast Givven, Chief Dragon Master, a spare wiry man with a flat crooked-nosed face, eyes black and blank as drops of ink on a plate. Habitually terse and tight-lipped, he waxed almost eloquent in opposition to the attack upon Banbeck Vale. "Look you, Ervis Carcolo, we are able to deploy a horde of Termagants, with sufficient Striding Murderers and Long-horned Murderers. But Blue Horrors, Fiends, and Juggers—no! We are lost if they trap us on the fells!"

"I do not plan to fight on the fells," said Carcolo. "I will force battle upon Joaz Banbeck. His Juggers and Fiends are useless on the cliffs. And in the matter of Blue Horrors we are almost his equal."

"You overlook a single difficulty," said Bast Givven.

"And what is this?"

"The improbability that Joaz Banbeck plans to permit all this. I allow him greater intelligence."

"Show me evidence!" charged Carcolo. "What I know of him suggests vacillation and stupidity! So we will strike—hard!" Carcolo smacked fist into palm. "Thus we will finish the haughty Banbecks!"

Bast Givven turned to go; Carcolo wrathfully called him back. "You show no enthusiasm for this campaign!"

"I know what our army can do and what it cannot

42

do," said Givven bluntly. "If Joaz Banbeck is the man you think he is, we might succeed. If he has even the sagacity of a pair of grooms I listened to ten minutes ago, we face disaster."

In a voice thick with rage, Carcolo said, "Return to your Fiends and Juggers. I want them quick as Termagants."

Bast Givven went his way. Carcolo jumped on a nearby Spider, kicked it with his heels. The creature sprang forward, halted sharply, twisted its long neck to look Carcolo in the face. Carcolo cried, "Hust, hust! Forward at speed, smartly now! Show these louts what snap and spirit means!" The Spider jumped ahead with such vehemence that Carcolo tumbled over backward, landing on his neck, where he lay groaning. Grooms came running, assisted him to a bench where he sat cursing in a steady low voice. A surgeon examined, pressed, prodded, recommended that Carcolo take to his couch, and administered a sedative potion.

Carcolo was carried to his apartments beneath the west wall of Happy Valley, placed under the care of his wives, and so slept for twenty hours. When he awoke the day was half gone. He wished to arise, but found himself too stiff to move, and groaning, lay back. Presently he called for Bast Givven, who appeared and listened without comment to Carcolo's adjurations. Evening arrived; the dragons returned to the barracks; there was nothing to do now but wait for daybreak.

During the long night Carcolo underwent a variety of treatments: massages, hot baths, infusions, and poultices. He exercised with diligence, and as the night reached its end, he declared himself fit. Overhead the star Coralyne vibrated poisonous colors: red, green, white, by far the brightest star of the cluster. Carcolo refused to look up at the star, but its radiance struck through the corners of his eyes whenever he walked on the valley floor.

Dawn approached. Carcolo planned to march at the earliest moment the dragons were manageable. A flickering to the east told of the oncoming dawn storm, still invisible across the horizon. With great caution the dragons were mustered from their barracks, and ordered into a marching column. There were almost three hundred Termagants, eighty-five Striding Murderers, as many Long-horned Murderers, a hundred Blue Horrors, fifty-two squat, immensely powerful Fiends, their tails tipped with spiked steel balls, and eighteen Juggers. They growled and muttered evilly among themselves, watching an opportunity to kick each other or to snip a leg from an unwary groom. Darkness stimulated their latent hatred for humanity, though they had been taught nothing of their past, nor the circumstances by which they had become enslaved.

The dawn lightning blazed and crackled, outlining the vertical steeples, the astonishing peaks of the Malheur Mountains. Overhead passed the storm, with wailing gusts of wind and thrashing banks of rain, and moved on toward Banbeck Vale. The east glowed with a gray-green pallor, and Carcolo gave the signal to march. Still stiff and sore he hobbled to his Spider, mounted, ordered the creature into a special and dramatic curvet. Carcolo had miscalculated; malice of the night still gripped the mind of the Spider. It ended its curvet with a lash of the neck which once again dashed Carcolo to the ground, where he lay half-mad with pain and frustration.

He tried to rise, collapsed; tried again, fainted. Five minutes he lay unconscious, then seemed to rouse himself by sheer force of will. "Lift me," he whispered huskily. "Tie me into the saddle. We must march." This being manifestly impossible, no one made a move. Carcolo raged, finally called hoarsely for Bast Givven. "Proceed; we cannot stop now. You must lead the troops."

Givven nodded glumly. This was an honor for which he had no stomach.

"You know the battle plan," wheezed Carcolo. "Circle north of the Fang, cross the Skanse with all speed, swing north around Blue Crevasse, then south along Banbeck Verge. There Joaz Banbeck may be expected to discover you, and you must deploy so that when he brings up his Juggers you can topple them back with Fiends. Avoid commiting our Juggers, harry him with Termagants, reserve the Murderers to strike wherever he reaches the edge. Do you understand me?"

"As you explain it, victory is certain," muttered Bast Givven.

"And so it is, unless you blunder grievously. Ah, my back! I can't move. While the great battle rages

I must sit by the brooder and watch eggs hatch! Now go! Strike hard for Happy Valley!"

Givven gave an order; the troops set forth. Termagants darted into the lead, followed by silken Striding Monsters and the heavier Long-horned Murderers, their fantastic chest-spikes tipped with steel. Behind came the ponderous Juggers, grunting, gurgling, teeth clashing together with the vibration of their steps. Flanking the Juggers marched the Fiends, carrying heavy cutlasses, flourishing their terminal steel balls as a scorpion carries his sting; then at the rear came the Blue Horrors, who were both massive and quick, good climbers, no less intelligent than the Termagants. To the flanks rode a hundred men; dragon masters, knights, fuglemen and cornets. They were armed with swords, pistols and large-bore blunderbusses.

Carcolo, on a stretcher, watched till the last of his forces had passed from view, then commanded himself carried back to the portal which led into the Happy Valley caves. Never before had the caves seemed so dingy and shallow. Sourly he eyed the straggle of huts along the cliff, built of rock, slabs of resin-impregnated lichen, canes bound with tar. With the Banbeck campaign at an end, he would set about cutting new chambers and halls into the cliff. The splendid decorations of Banbeck Village were well known; Happy Valley would be even more magnificent. The halls would glow with opal and nacre, silver and gold. And yet, to what end? If events went as planned, there was his great dream in prospect.

And then, what consequences a few paltry decorations in the tunnels of Happy Valley?

Groaning he allowed himself to be laid on his couch, and entertained himself picturing the progress of his troops. By now they should be working down from Dangle Ridge, circling the mile-high Fang. He tentatively stretched his arms, worked his legs. His muscles protested, pain shot back and forth along his body—but it seemed as if the injuries were less than before. By now the army would be mounting the ramparts which rimmed that wide area of upland fell known as the Skanse. The surgeon brought Carcolo a potion; he drank and slept, to awake with a start. What was the time? His troops might well have joined battle! He ordered himself carried to the outer portal; then, still dissatisfied, commanded his servants to transport him across the valley to the new dragon brooder, the walkway of which commanded a view up and down the valley. Despite the protests of his wives, here he was conveyed, and made as comfortable as bruises and sprains permitted.

He settled himself for an indeterminate wait, but news was not long in coming.

Down the North Trail came a cornet on a foam-bearded Spider. Carcolo sent a groom to intercept him, and heedless of aches and pains, raised himself from his couch. The cornet threw himself off his mount, staggered up the ramp, sagged exhausted against the rail.

"Ambush!" he panted. "Bloody disaster!"

"Ambush?" groaned Carcolo in a hollow voice. "Where?"

"As we mounted the Skanse Ramparts. They waited till our Termagants and Murderers were over, then charged with Horrors, Fiends and Juggers. They cut us apart, drove us back, then rolled boulders on our Juggers! Our army is broken!"

Carcolo sank back on the couch, lay staring at the sky. "How many are lost?"

"I do not know. Givven called the retreat; we withdrew in the best style possible."

Carcolo lay as if comatose, the cornet flung himself down on a bench.

A column of dust appeared to the north, which presently dissolved and separated to reveal a number of Happy Valley dragons. All were wounded; they marched, hopped, limped, dragged themselves at random, croaking, glaring, bugling. First came a group of Termagants, darting ugly heads from side to side; then a pair of Blue Horrors, brachs twisting and clasping almost like human arms; then a Jugger, massive, toad-like, legs splayed out in weariness. Even as it neared the barracks it toppled, fell with a thud to lay still, legs and talons jutting into the air.

Down from the North Trail rode Bast Givven, dust-stained and haggard. He dismounted from his drooping Spider, mounted the ramp. With a wrenching effort, Carcolo once more raised himself on the couch.

Givven reported in a raised voice so even and light as to seem careless, but even the insensitive Carcolo was not deceived. He asked in puzzlement, "Exactly where did the ambush occur?"

"We mounted the Ramparts by way of Chloris Ravine. Where the Skanse falls off into the ravine a porphyry outcrop juts up and over. Here they awaited us."

Carcolo hissed through his teeth. "Amazing."

Bast Givven gave the faintest of nods.

Carcolo said, "Assume that Joaz Banbeck set forth during the dawn-storm, an hour earlier than I would think possible; assume that he forced his troops at a run. How could he reach the Ramparts before us?"

"By my reckoning," said Givven, "ambush was no threat until we had crossed the Skanse. I had planned to patrol Barchback, all the way down Blue Fell, and across Blue Crevasse."

Carcolo gave somber agreement. "How then did Joaz Banbeck bring his troops to the Ramparts so soon?"

Givven turned, looked up the valley, where wounded dragons and men still straggled down the North Trail. "I have no idea."

"A drug?" puzzled Carcolo. "A potion to pacify the dragons? Could he have made bivouac on the Skanse the whole night long?"

"The last is possible," admitted Givven grudgingly. "Under Barch Spike are empty caves. If he quartered his troops there during the night, then he had only to march across the Skanse to waylay us."

Carcolo grunted. "Perhaps we have underestimated

Joaz Banbeck." He sank back on his couch with a groan. "Well then, what are our losses?"

The reckoning made dreary news. Of the already inadequate squad of Juggers, only six remained. From a force of fifty-two Fiends, forty survived and of these five were sorely wounded. Termagants, Blue Horrors and Murderers had suffered greatly. A large number had been torn apart in the first onslaught, many others had been toppled down the Ramparts to strew their armored husks through the detritus. Of the hundred men, twelve had been killed by bullets, another fourteen by dragon attack; a score more were wounded in various degrees.

Carcolo lay back, his eyes closed, his mouth working feebly.

"The terrain alone saved us," said Givven. "Joaz Banbeck refused to commit his troops to the ravine. If there were any tactical error on either side, it was his. He brought an insufficiency of Termagants and Blue Horrors."

"Small comfort," growled Carcolo. "Where is the balance of the army?"

"We have good position on Dangle Ridge. We have seen none of Banbeck's scouts, either man or Termagant, and he may conceivably believe we have returned to the valley. In any event his main forces were still collected on the Skanse."

Carcolo, by an enormous effort raised himself to his feet. He tottered across the walkway, looked down into the dispensary. Five Fiends crouched in vats of balsam, muttering, sighing. A Blue Horror hung in a sling, whining as surgeons cut broken fragments of armor from its gray flesh. As Carcolo watched, one of the Fiends raised itself high on its anterior legs, foam gushing from its gills. It cried out in a peculiar poignant tone, fell back dead into the balsam.

Carcolo turned back to Givven. "This is what you must do. Joaz Banbeck surely has sent forth patrols. Retire along Dangle Ridge, then taking all concealment from the patrols, swing up into one of the Despire Cols—Tourmaline Col will serve. This is my reasoning. Banbeck will assume that you are retiring to Happy Valley, he will hurry south behind the Fang, to attack as you come down off Dangle Ridge. As he passed below Tourmaline Col, you have the advantage, and may well destroy Joaz Banbeck with all his troops."

Bast Givven shook his head decisively. "What if his patrols locate us in spite of our precautions? He need only follow our tracks to bottle us into Tourmaline Col, with no escape except over Mount Despoire or out on Starbreak Fell. And if we venture out on Starbreak Fell his Juggers will destroy us in minutes."

Ervis Carcolo sagged back down upon the couch. "Bring the troops back to Happy Valley. We will await another occasion."

CHAPTER 6

Cut into the cliff south of the crag which housed Joaz's apartments was a large chamber known as Kergan's Hall. The proportions of the room, the simplicity and lack of ornament, the massive antique furniture contributed to the sense of lingering personality, as well as an odor unique to the room. The odor exhaled from naked stone walls, the petrified moss parquetry, old wood—a rough ripe redolence which Joaz had always disliked, together with every other aspect of the room. The dimensions seemed arrogant in their extent, the lack of ornament impressed him as rude, if not brutal. One day it occurred to Joaz that he disliked not the room but Kergan Banbeck himself, together with the entire system of overblown legends which surrounded him.

The room nevertheless in many respects was pleasant. Three tall groined windows overlooked the vale. The casements were set with small square panes of green-blue glass in mutins of black ironwood. The ceiling likewise was paneled in wood, and here a certain amount of the typical Banbeck intricacy had been permitted. There were mock pilaster capitals with gargoyle heads, a frieze carved with conventionalized fern-fronds. The furniture consisted of three

52

pieces—two tall carved chairs and a massive table, all polished dark wood, all of enormous antiquity.

Joaz had found a use for the room. The table supported a carefully detailed relief map of the district, on a scale of three inches to the mile. At the center was Banbeck Vale, on the right hand Happy Valley, separated by a turmoil of crags and chasms, cliffs, spikes, walls and five titanic peaks. Mount Gethron to the south, Mount Despoire in the center, Barch Spike, the Fang and Mount Halcyon to the north.

At the front of Mount Gethron lay the High Jambles, then Starbreak Fell extended to Mount Despoire and Barch Spike. Beyond Mount Despoire, between the Skanse Ramparts and Barchback, the Skanse reached all the way to the tormented basalt ravines and bluffs at the foot of Mount Halcyon.

As Joaz stood studying the map, into the room came Phade, mischievously quiet. But Joaz sensed her nearness by the scent of incense, in the smoke of which she had steeped herself before seeking out Joaz. She wore a traditional holiday costume of Banbeck maidens—a tight-fitting sheath of dragon intestine, with muffs of brown fur at neck, elbows and knees. A tall cylindrical hat, notched around the upper edge, perched on her rich brown curls, and from the top of this hat soared a red plume.

Joaz feigned unconsciousness of her presence; she came up behind him to tickle his neck with the fur of her neckpiece. Joaz pretended stolid indifference; Phade, not at all decieved, put on a face of woeful concern. "Must we all be slain? How goes the war?"

"For Banbeck Vale the war goes well. For poor Ervis Carcolo and Happy Valley the war goes ill indeed."

"You plan his destruction," Phade intoned in a voice of hushed accusation. "You will kill him! Poor Ervis Carcolo!"

"He deserves no better."

"But what will befall Happy Valley?"

Joaz Banbeck shrugged. "Changes for the better."

"Will you seek to rule?"

"Not I."

"Think!" whispered Phade. "Joaz Banbeck, Tyrant of Banbeck Vale, Happy Valley, Phosphur Gulch, Glore, the Tarn, Clewhaven and the Great Northern Rift."

"Not I," said Joaz. "Perhaps you would rule in my stead?"

"Oh! Indeed! What changes there would be! I'd dress the sacerdotes in red and yellow ribbons. I'd order them to sing and dance and drink May wine; the dragons I'd send south to Arcady, except for a few gentle Termagants to nursemaid the children. And no more of these furious battles. I'd burn the armor and break the swords, I'd—"

"My dear little flutterbug," said Joaz with a laugh. "What a swift reign you'd have indeed!"

"Why swift? Why not forever? If men had no means to fight—"

"And when the Basics came down, you'd throw garlands around their necks?"

"Pah. They shall never be seen again. What do they gain by molesting a few remote valleys?"

"Who knows what they gain? We are free men—perhaps the last free men in the universe. Who knows? And will they be back? Coralyne is bright in the sky!"

Phade became suddenly interested in the relief map. "And your current war—dreadful! Will you attack, will you defend?"

"This depends on Ervis Carcolo," said Joaz. "I need only wait till he exposes himself." Looking down at the map he added thoughtfully, "He is clever enough to do me damage, unless I move with care."

"And what if the Basics come while you bicker with Carcolo?"

Joaz smiled. "Perhaps we shall all flee to the Jambles. Perhaps we shall all fight."

"I will fight beside you," declared Phade, striking a brave attitude. "We will attack the great Basic spaceship, braving the heat rays, fending off the power bolts. We will storm to the very portal, we will pull the nose of the first marauder who shows himself!"

"At one point your otherwise sage strategy falls short," said Joaz. "How does one find the nose of a Basic?"

"In that case," said Phade, "we shall seize their—" She turned her head at the sound in the hall. Joaz strode across the room, flung back the door. Old Rife the porter sidled forward. "You told me to call when

55

either the bottle overturned or broke. Well, it's done both, and irreparably, not five minutes ago."

Joaz pushed past Rife, ran down the corridor. "What means this?" demanded Phade. "Rife, what have you said to disturb him?"

Rife shook his head fretfully. "I am as perplexed as you. A bottle is pointed out to me. 'Watch this bottle day and night.' So I am commanded. And also, 'When the bottle breaks or tips, call me at once.' I tell myself that here in all truth is a sinecure. And I wonder, does Joaz consider me so senile that I will rest content with a make-work task such as watching a bottle? I am old, my jaws tremble, but I am not witless. To my surprise the bottle breaks! The explanation admittedly is workaday: a fall to the floor. Nevertheless, without knowledge of what it all means, I obey orders and so have notified Joaz Banbeck."

Phade had been squirming impatiently. "Where then is this bottle?"

"In the studio of Joaz Banbeck."

Phade ran off as swiftly as the tight sheath about her thighs permitted. She passed through a transverse tunnel, across Kergan's Way by a covered bridge, then up at a slant toward Joaz's apartments.

Down the long hall ran Phade, through the anteroom where a bottle lay shattered on the floor, into the studio, where she halted in astonishment. No one was to be seen. She noticed a section of shelving which stood at an angle. Quietly, timorously, she stole across the room, peered down into the workshop.

The scene was an odd one. Joaz stood negligently,

smiling a cool smile, as across the room a naked sacerdote gravely sought to shift a barrier which had sprung down across an area of the wall. But the gate was cunningly locked in place and the sacerdote's efforts were to no avail. He turned, glanced briefly at Joaz, then started for the exit into the studio.

Phade sucked in her breath, backed away.

The sacerdote came out into the studio, started for the door.

"Just a moment," said Joaz. "I wish to speak to you."

The sacerdote paused, turned his head in mild inquiry. He was a young man, his face bland, blank, almost beautiful. Fine transparent skin stretched over his pale bones; his eyes, wide, blue, innocent, seemed to stare without focus. He was delicate of frame, sparsely fleshed; his hands were thin, with fingers trembling in some kind of nervous imbalance. Down his back, almost to his waist, hung the mane of long light-brown hair.

Joaz seated himself with ostentatious deliberation, never taking his eyes from the sacerdote. Presently he spoke in a voice pitched at an ominous level. "I find your conduct far from ingratiating." This was a declaration requiring no response, and the sacerdote made none.

"Please sit," said Joaz. He indicated a bench. "You have a great deal of explaining to do."

Was it Phade's imagination? Or did a spark of something like wild amusement flicker and die almost instantaneously in the sacerdote's eyes? But again he made no response. Joaz, adapting to the peculiar rules by which communication with the sacerdotes must be conducted, asked, "Do you care to sit?"

"It is immaterial," said the sacerdote. "Since I am standing now, I will stand."

Joaz rose to his feet and performed an act without precedent. He pushed the bench behind the sacerdote, rapped the back of the knobby knees, thrust the sacerdote firmly down upon the bench. "Since you are sitting now," said Joaz, "You might as well sit."

With gentle dignity the sacerdote regained his feet. "I shall stand."

Joaz shrugged. "As you wish. I intend to ask you some questions. I hope that you will co-operate and answer with precision."

The sacerdote blinked owlishly.

"Will you do so?"

"Certainly. I prefer, however, to return the way I came."

Joaz ignored the remark. "First," he asked, "why do you come to my study?"

The sacerdote spoke carefully, in the voice of one talking to a child. "Your language is vague; I am confused and must not respond, since I am vowed to give only truth to anyone who requires it."

Joaz settled himself in his chair. "There is no jurry. I am ready for a long discussion. Let me ask you then —did you have impulses which you can explain to me, which persuaded or impelled you to come to my studio?"

"Yes."

"How many of these impulses did you recognize?"

"I don't know."

"More than one?"

"Perhaps."

"Less than ten?"

"I don't know."

"Hmm . . . Why are you uncertain?"

"I am not uncertain."

"Then why can't you specify the number as I requested?"

"There is no such number."

"I see. You mean, possibly, that there are several elements of a single motive which directed your brain to signal your muscles in order that they might carry you here?"

"Possibly."

Joaz's thin lips twisted in a faint smile of triumph. "Can you describe an element of the eventual motive?"

"Yes."

"Do so, then."

There was an imperative, against which the sacerdote was proof. Any form of coercion known to Joaz —fire, sword, thirst, mutilation—these to a sacerdote were no more than inconveniences; he ignored them as if they did not exist. His personal inner world was the single world of reality; either acting upon or reacting against the affairs of the Utter Men demeaned him, absolute passivity, absolute candor were his necessary courses of action. Understanding something of this, Joaz rephrased his command. "Can you think of an element of the motive which impelled you to come here?"

"Yes."

"What is it?"

"A desire to wander about."

"Can you think of another?"

"Yes."

"What is it?"

"A desire to exercise myself by walking."

"I see. Incidentally, are you trying to evade answering my questions?"

"I answer such questions as you put to me. So long as I do so, so long as I open my mind to all who seek knowledge—for this is our creed—there can be no question of evasion."

"So you say. However, you have not provided me an answer that I find satisfactory."

The sacerdote's reply to the comment was an almost imperceptible widening of the pupils.

"Very well then," said Joaz Banbeck. "Can you think of another element of this complex motive we have been discussing?"

"Yes."

"What is it?"

"I am interested in antiques. I came to your study to admire your relics of the old worlds."

"Indeed?" Joaz raised his eyebrows. "I am lucky to possess such fascinating treasures. Which of my antiques interests you particularly?"

"Your books, your maps, your great globe of the Arch-world."

"The Arch-world? Eden?"

"This is one of its names."

Joaz pursed his lips. "So you come here to study my antiques. Well then, what other elements to this motive exist?"

The sacerdote hesitated an instant. "It was suggested to me that I come here."

"By whom?"

"By the Demie."

"Why did he so suggest?"

"I am uncertain."

"Can you conjecture?"

"Yes."

"What are these conjectures?"

The sacerdote made a small bland gesture with the fingers of one hand. "The Demie might wish to become an Utter Man, and so seeks to learn the principles of your existence. Or the Demie might wish to change the trade articles. The Demie might be fascinated by my description of your antiques. Or the Demie might be curious regarding the focus of your vision panels. Or—"

"Enough. Which of these conjectures, and of other conjectures you have not yet divulged, do you consider most probable?"

"None."

Joaz raised his eyebrows once more. "How do you justify this?"

"Since any desired number of conjectures can be formed, the denominator of any probability-ratio is variable and the entire concept becomes meaningless.

Joaz grinned wearily. "Of the conjectures which to this moment have occurred to you, which do you regard as the most likely?"

"I suspect that the Demie might think it desirable that I come here to stand."

"What do you achieve by standing?"

"Nothing."

"Then the Demie does not send you here to stand."

To Joaz's assertion, the sacerdote made no comment.

Joaz framed a question with great care. "What do you believe that the Demie hopes you will achieve by coming here to stand?"

"I believe that he wishes me to learn how Utter Men think."

"And you learn how I think by coming here?"

"I am learning a great deal."

"How does it help you?"

"I don't know."

"How many times have you visited my study?"

"Seven times."

"Why were you chosen specially to come?"

"The synod has approved my *tand*. I may well be the next Demie."

Joaz spoke over his shoulder to Phade. "Brew tea." He turned back to the sacerdote. "What is a *tand*?"

The sacerdote took a deep breath. "My *tand* is the representation of my soul."

"Hmm. What does it look like?"

The sacerdote's expression was unfathomable. "It cannot be described."

"Do I have one?"

"No."

Joaz shrugged. "Then you can read my thoughts."

Silence.

"Can you read my thoughts?"

"Not well."

"Why should you wish to read my thoughts?"

"We are alive in the universe together. Since we are not permitted to act, we are obliged to know."

Joaz smiled skeptically. "How does knowledge help you, if you will not act upon what you know?"

"Events follow the Rationale, as water drains into a hollow and forms a pool."

"Bah!" said Joaz, in sudden irritation. "Your doctrine commits you to non-interference in our affairs, nevertheless you allow your 'Rationale' to create conditions by which events are influenced. Is this correct?"

"I am not sure. We are a passive people."

"Still, your Demie must have had a plan in mind when he sent you here. Is this not correct?"

"I cannot say."

Joaz veered to a new line of questioning. "Where does the tunnel behind my workshop lead?"

"Into a cavern."

Phade set a silver pot before Joaz. He poured, sipped reflectively. Of contests there were numberless varieties; he and the sacerdote were engaged in a hide-and-seek game of words and ideas. The sacerdote was schooled in patience and supple evasions, to counter which Joaz could bring pride and determination. The sacerdote was handicapped by an innate necessity to speak truth; Joaz, on the other hand, must grope like a man blindfolded, unacquainted with the goal he sought, ignorant of the prize to be won. Very well, thought Joaz, let us continue. We shall see whose nerves fray first. He offered tea to the sacerdote, who refused with a shake of the head so quick and of such small compass as to seem a shudder.

Joaz made a gesture signifying it was all the same to him. "Should you desire sustenance or drink," he said, "please let it be known. I enjoy our conversation so inordinately that I fear I may prolong it to the limits of your patience. Surely you would prefer to sit?"

"No."

"As you wish. Well then, back to our discussion. This cavern you mentioned—is it inhabited by sacerdotes?"

"I fail to understand your question."

"Do sacerdotes use the cavern?"

"Yes."

Eventually, fragment by fragment, Joaz extracted the information that the cavern connected with a series of chambers, in which the sacerdotes smelted metal, boiled glass, ate, slept, performed their rituals. At one time there had been an opening into Banbeck Vale, but long ago this had been blocked. Why? There were wars throughout the cluster; bands of defeated men were taking refuge upon Aerlith, settling n rifts and valleys. The sacerdotes preferred a detached existence and had shut their caverns away from sight. Where was this opening? The sacerdote seemed vague, indefinite. Somewhere to the north end of the valley. Behind Banbeck Jambles? Possibly. But trading between men and sacerdotes was conducted at a cave entrance below Mount Gethron. Why? A matter of usage, declared the sacerdote. In addition this location was more readily accessible to Happy Valley and Phosphor Gulch. How many sacerdotes lived in these caves? Uncertainty. Some might have died, others might have been born. Approximately how many this morning? Perhaps five hundred.

At this juncture the sacerdote was swaying and Joaz was hoarse. "Back to your motive—or the elements of your motives—for coming to my studio. Are they connected in any manner with the star Coralyne, and a possible new coming of the Basics, or the grephs, as they were formerly called?"

Again the sacerdote seemed to hesitate. Then, "Yes."

"Will the sacerdotes help us against the Basics, should they come?"

"No." This answer was terse and definite.

"But I assume that the sacerdotes wish the Basics driven off?"

No answer.

Joaz rephrased his words. "Do the sacerdotes wish the Basics repelled from Aerlith?"

"The Rationale bids us stand aloof from affairs of men and non-men alike."

Joaz curled his lip. "Suppose the Basics invade your caves, dragged you off to Coralyne planet, then what?"

The sacerdote almost seemed to laugh. "The question cannot be answered."

"Would you resist the Basics if they made the attempt?"

"I cannot answer your question."

Joaz laughed. "But the answer is not so?"

The sacerdote assented.

"Do you have weapons, then?"

The sacerdote's mild blue eyes seemed to droop. Secrecy? Fatigue? Joaz repeated the question.

"Yes," said the sacerdote. His knees sagged, but he snapped them tight.

"What kind of weapons?"

"Numberless varieties. Projectiles, such as rocks. Piercing weapons, such as broken sticks. Cutting and slashing weapons such as cooking utensils." His voice began to fade as if he were moving away. "Poisons—arsenic, sulfur, triventidum, acid, black-spore. Burning weapons, such as torches and lenses to focus the sunlight. Weapons to suffocate—ropes, nooses, slings and cords. Cisterns, to drown the enemy. . . ."

"Sit down, rest," Joaz urged him. "Your inventory interests me, but its total effect seems inadequate. Have you other weapons which might decisively repel the Basics should they attack you?"

The question, by design, or chance, was never answered. The sacerdote sank to his knees, slowly, as if praying. He fell forward on his face, then sprawled to the side. Joaz sprang forward, yanked up the drooping head by its hair. The eyes half-open, revealed a hideous white expanse. "Speak!" croaked Joaz. "Answer my last question! Do you have weapons—or a weapon—to repel a Basic attack?"

The pallid lips moved. "I don't know."

Joaz frowned, peered into the waxen face, drew back in bewilderment. "The man is dead."

Phade looked up from drowsing on a couch, face pink, hair tossed. "You have killed him!" she cried in a voice of hushed horror.

"No. He has died—or caused himself to die."

Phade staggered blinking across the room, sidled close to Joaz, who pushed her absently away. Phade scowled, shrugged, and then as Joaz paid her no heed, marched from the room.

Joaz sat back, staring at the limp body. "He did not tire," muttered Joaz, "until I verged upon secrets."

Presently he jumped to his feet, went to the entry hall, sent Rife to fetch a barber. An hour later the corpse, stripped of hair, lay on a wooden pallet covered by a sheet, and Joaz held in his hands a rude wig fashioned from the long hair.

The barber departed; servants carried away the corpse. Joaz stood alone in his studio, tense and light-headed. He removed his garments, to stand naked as the sacerdote. Gingerly he drew the wig across his scalp and examined himself in the mirror. To a casual eye, where the difference? Something was lacking. The torc. Joaz fitted it about his neck, once more examined his reflection, with dubious satisfaction.

He entered the workshop, hesitated, disengaged the trap, cautiously pulled away the stone slab. On hands and knees he peered into the tunnel, and since it was dark, held forward a glass vial of luminescent algae. In the faint light the tunnel seemed empty. Irrevocably putting down his fears, Joaz clambered through the opening. The tunnel was narrow and low; Joaz moved forward tentatively, nerves thrilling with wariness. He stopped often to listen, but heard nothing but the whisper of his own pulse.

After perhaps a hundred yards the tunnel broke out into a natural cavern. Joaz stopped, stood indecisively, straining his ears through the gloom. Luminescent vials fixed to the walls at irregular intervals provided a measure of light, enough to delineate the direction of the cavern, which seemed to be north, parallel to the length of the valley. Joaz set forth once again, halting to listen every few yards. To the best of his knowledge the sacerdotes were a mild unaggressive folk, but they were also intensely secretive. How would they respond to the presence of an interloper? Joaz could not be sure, and proceeded with great caution.

The cavern rose, fell, widened, narrowed. Joaz presently came upon evidences of use—small cubicles, hollowed into the walls, lit by candelabra holding tall vials of luminous stuff. In two of the cubicles Joaz came upon sacerdotes, the first asleep on a reed rug; the second sitting cross-legged, gazing fixedly at a contrivance of twisted metal rods. They gave Joaz no attention; he continued with a more confident step.

The cave sloped downward, widened like a cornucopia, suddenly broke into a cavern so enormous that Joaz thought for a startled instant that he had stepped out into the night. The ceiling reached beyond the flicker of the myriad of lamps, fires and glowing vials. Ahead and to the left smelters and forges seemed to be in operation; then a twist in the cavern wall obscured something of the view. Joaz glimpsed a tiered tubular construction which seemed to be some sort of workshop, for a large number of sacerdotes were occupied at complicated tasks. To the right was a stack of bales; a row of bins contained goods of unknown nature. Joaz for the first time saw sacerdote women. They were neither the nymphs nor the half-human witches of popular legend. Like the men they seemed pallid and frail, with sharply defined features; like the men they moved with care and deliberation; and like the men they wore only their waist-long hair. There was little conversation and no laughter: rather an atmosphere of not unhappy placidity and concentration. The cavern exuded a sense of time, of use and custom. The stone floor was polished by endless padding of bare feet; the exhalations of many generations had stained the walls.

No one heeded Joaz. He moved slowly forward, keeping to the shadows, and paused under the stack of bales. To the right the cavern dwindled by irregular proportions into a vast horizontal funnel receding, twisting, telescoping, losing all reality in the dim light.

Joaz searched the entire sweep of vast cavern. Where would be the armory, with the weapons whose existence the sacerdote, by the very act of dying, had assured him? Joaz turned his attention once more to the left, straining to see detail in the odd tiered workshop which rose fifty feet from the stone floor. A strange edifice, thought Joaz, craning his neck; one whose nature he could not entirely comprehend. But every aspect of the great cavern—so close beside Banbeck Vale and so remote—was strange and marvelous. Weapons? They might be anywhere; certainly he dared seek no further for them. There was nothing more he could learn without risk of discovery. He turned back the way he had come—up the dim passage, past the occasional side cubicles, where the two sacerdotes remained as he had found them before—the one asleep, the other intent on the contrivance of twisted metal. He plodded on and on. Had he come so far? Where was the fissure which led to his own apartment? Had he passed it by, must he search? Panic rose in his throat, but he continued, watching carefully. There, he had not gone wrong! There it opened to his right, a fissure almost dear and familiar. He plunged into it, walked with long loping strides, like a man under water, holding his luminous tube ahead. An apparition rose before him, a tall white shape. Joaz stood rigid. The gaunt figure bore down upon him. Joaz pressed against the wall. The figure stalked forward, and suddenly shrank to human scale.

It was the young sacerdote whom Joaz had shorn and left for dead. He confronted Joaz, mild blue eyes bright with reproach and contempt. "Give me my torc."

With numb fingers Joaz removed the golden collar. The sacerdote took it, but made no move to clasp it upon himself. He looked at the hair which weighed heavy upon Joaz's scalp. With a foolish grimace Joaz doffed the disheveled wig, proffered it. The sacerdote sprang back as if Joaz had become a cave goblin. Sidling past, as far from Joaz as the wall of the passage allowed, he paced swiftly off down the tunnel. Joaz dropped the wig to the floor, stared down at the unkempt pile of hair. He turned, looked after the sacerdote, a pallid figure which soon became one with the murk. Slowly Joaz continued up the tunnel. There —an oblong blank of light, the opening to his workshop. He crawled through back to the real world. Savagely, with all his strength, he thrust the slab back in the hole, slammed down the gate which originally had trapped the sacerdote.

Joaz's garments lay where he had tossed them. Wrapping himself in a cloak he went to the outer door, looked forth into the anteroom, where Rife sat dozing. Joaz snapped his fingers. "Fetch masons, with mortar, steel and stone."

Joaz bathed with diligence, rubbing himself time after time with emulsion, rinsing and re-rinsing himself. Emerging from the bath he took the waiting masons into his workshop, ordered the sealing of the hole.

Then he took himself to his couch. Sipping a cup of wine, he let his mind rove and wander. Recollection became reverie, reverie became dream. Joaz once again traversed the tunnel, on feet light as thistledown, down the long cavern, and the sacerdotes in their cubicles now raised their heads to look after him. At last he stood in the entrance to the great underground void, and once more looked right and left in awe. Now he drifted across the floor, past sacerdotes laboring earnestly over fires and anvils. Sparks rose from retorts, blue gas flickered above melting metal.

Joaz moved beyond to a small chamber cut into the stone. Here sat an old man, thin as a pole, his waist-long mane of hair snow-white. The man examined Joaz with fathomless blue eyes, and spoke, but his voice was muffled, inaudible. He spoke again; the words rang loud in Joaz's mind.

"I bring you here to caution you, lest you do us harm, and with no profit to yourself. The weapon you seek is both non-existent and beyond your imagination. Put it outside your ambition."

By great effort Joaz managed to stammer. "The young sacerdote made no denial; this weapon must exist!"

"Only within the narrow limits of special interpretation. The lad can speak no more than the literal truth, nor can he act with other than grace. How can you wonder why we hold ourselves apart? You utter folk find purity incomprehensible; you thought to advantage yourself, but achieved nothing but an exercise in rat-like stealth. Lest you try again with greater boldness I must abase myself to set matters correctly. I assure you, this so-called weapon is absolutely beyond your control."

First shame, then indignation came over Joaz; he cried out, "You do not understand my urgencies! Why should I act differently? Coralyne is close; the Basics are at hand. Are you not men? Why will you not help us defend the planet?"

The Demie shook his head, and the white hair rippled with hypnotic slowness. "I quote you the Rationale: passivity, complete and absolute. This implies solitude, sanctity, quiescence, peace. Can you imagine the anguish I risk in speaking to you? I intervene, I interfere, at vast pain of the spirit. Let there be an end to it. We have made free with your studio, doing you no harm, offering you no indignity. You have paid a visit to our hall, demeaning a noble young man in the process. Let us be quits, let there be no further spying on either side. Do you agree?"

Joaz heard his voice respond, quite without his conscious prompting: it sounded more nasal and shrill than he liked. "You offer this agreement now when you have learned your fill of my secrets, but I know none of yours."

The Demie's face seemed to recede and quiver. Joaz read contempt, and in his sleep he tossed and twitched. He made an effort to speak in a voice of calm reason. "Come, we are men together; why should we be at odds? Let us share our secrets, let each help the other. Examine my archives, my cases, my relics at your leisure, and then allow me to study this existent but non-existent weapon. I swear it shall be used only against the Basics, for the protection of both of us."

The Demie's eyes sparkled. "No."

"Why not?" argued Joaz. "Surely you wish us no harm?"

"We are detached and passionless. We await your extinction. You are the Utter Men, and the last of humanity. And when you are gone, your dark thoughts and grim plots will be gone; murder and pain and malice will be gone."

"I cannot believe this," said Joaz. "There may be no men in the cluster, but what of the universe? The Old Rule reached far; sooner or later men will return to Aerlith."

The Demie's voice became plangent. "Do you think we speak only from faith? Do you doubt our knowledge?"

"The universe is large. The Old Rule reached far."

"The last men dwell on Aerlith," said the Demie. "The Utter men and the sacerdotes. You shall pass; we will carry forth the Rationale like a banner of glory, through all the worlds of the sky."

"And how will you transport yourselves on this mission?" Joaz asked cunningly. "Can you fly to the stars as naked as you walk the fells?"

"There will be means. Time is long."

"For your purposes, the time needs to be long. Even on the Coralyne planets there are men. Enslaved, re-shaped in body and mind, but men. What of them? It seems that you are wrong, that you are guided by faith indeed."

The Demie said mildly, "Facts can never be rec-"Are these not facts?" asked Joaz. "How do you reconcile them with your faith?"

The Demie said mildly, "'facts can never be reconciled with faith. By our faith, these men, if they exist, will also pass. Time is long; Oh, the worlds of brightness: they await us!"

"It is clear," said Joaz, "that you ally yourselves with the Basics, that you hope for our destruction, and this can only change our attitudes toward you. I fear that Ervis Carcolo was right and I wrong."

"We remain passive," said the Demie. His face wavered, seemed to swim with mottled colors. "Without emotion, we will stand witness to the passing of the Utter men, neither helping nor hindering."

Joaz spoke in fury: "Your faith, your Rationale—whatever you call it—misleads you. I make this threat —if you fail to help us, you will suffer as we suffer."

"We are passive, we are indifferent."

"What of your children? The Basics make no difference between us. They will herd you to their pens as readily as they do us. Why should we fight to protect you?"

The Demie's face faded, became splotched with fog, transparent mist; his eyes glowed like rotten meat. "We need no protection," he howled. "We are secure."

"You will suffer our fate," cried Joaz, "I promise you this!"

The Demie collapsed suddenly into a small dry husk, like a dead mosquito; with incredible speed, Joaz fled back through the caves, the tunnels, up through his workroom, his studio, into his bedchamber where now he jerked upright, eyes starting, throat distended, mouth dry.

The door opened; Rife's head appeared. "Did you call, sir?"

Joaz raised himself on his elbows, looked around the room. "No. I did not call."

Rife withdrew. Joaz settled back on the couch, lay staring at the ceiling. He had dreamed a most peculiar dream. Dream? A synthesis of his own imaginings? Or, in all verity, a confrontation and exchange between two minds? Impossible to decide, and perhaps irrelevant; the event carried its own conviction. Joaz swung his legs over the side of the couch, blinked at the floor. Dream or colloquy, it was all the same. He rose to his feet, donned sandals and a robe of yellow fur, limped morosely up to the Council Room and stepped out on a sunny balcony.

The day was two-thirds over. Shadows hung dense along the western cliffs. Right and left stretched Banbeck Vale. Never had it seemed more prosperous or more fruitful, and never before unreal, as if he were a stranger to the planet. He looked north along the great bulwark of stone which rose sheer to Banbeck Verge. This too was unreal, a facade behind which lived the sacerdotes. He gauged the rock face, superimposing a mental projection of the great cavern.

The cliff toward the north end of the vale must be scarcely more than a shell!

Joaz turned his attention to the exercise field, where Juggers were thudding briskly through defensive evolutions. How strange was the quality of life, which had produced Basic and Jugger, sacerdote and himself. He thought of Ervis Carcolo, and wrestled with sudden exasperation. Carcolo was a distraction most unwelcome at the present time; there would be no tolerance when Carcolo was finally brought to account. A light step behind him, the pressure of fur, the touch of gay hands, the scent of incense. Joaz's tensions melted. If there were no such creatures as minstrel-maidens, it would be necessary to invent them.

Deep under Banbeck Scarp, in a cubicle lit by a twelve-vial candelabra, a naked white-haired man sat quietly. On a pedestal at the level of his eyes rested his *tand*, an intricate construction of gold rods and silver wire, woven and bent seemingly at random. The fortuitousness of the design, however, was only apparent. Each curve symbolized an aspect of Final Sentience; the shadow cast upon the wall represented the Rationale, ever-shifting, always the same.

The object was sacred to the sacerdotes, and served as a source of revelation. There was never an end to the study of the *tand*: new intuitions were continually derived from some heretofore overlooked relationship of angle and curve. The nomenclature was elaborate: each part, juncture, sweep and twist had its name; each aspect of the relationships between the various parts was likewise categorized. Such was the cult of the *tand*: abstruse, exacting, without compromise. At his puberty rites the young sacerdote might study the original *tand* for as long as he chose; each must construct a duplicate *tand*, relying upon memory alone. Then occurred the most significant event of his lifetime: The viewing of his *tand* by a synod of elders. In awesome stillness, for hours at a time they would ponder his creation, weigh the infinitesimal variations of proportion, radius, sweep and angle. So they would infer the initiate's quality, judge his personal attributes, determine his understanding of Final Sentience, the Rationale and the Basis.

Occasionally the testimony of the *tand* revealed a character so tainted as to be reckoned intolerable; the vile *tand* would be cast into a furnace, the molten metal consigned to a latrine, the unlucky initiate expelled to the face of the planet, to live on his own terms.

The naked white-haired Demie, contemplating his own beautiful *tand*, sighed, moved restlessly. He had been visited by an influence so ardent, so passionate, so simultaneously cruel and tender, that his mind was oppressed. Unbidden, into his mind, came a dark seep of doubt. Can it be, he asked himself, that we have insensibly wandered from the true Rationale? Do we study our *tands* with blinded eyes? How to know, oh how to know! All is relative ease and facility in orthodoxy, yet how can it be denied that good is in itself undeniable? Absolutes are the most uncertain of all formulations, while the uncertainties are the most real.

Twenty miles over the mountains, in the long pale light of the Aerlith afternoon, Ervis Carcolo planned his own plans. "By daring, by striking hard, by cutting deep I can defeat him! In resolve, in courage, in endurance, I am more than his equal. Not again will he trick me, to slaughter my dragons and kill my men! Oh, Joaz Banbeck, how I will pay you for your deceit!" He raised his arms in wrath. "Oh Joaz Banbeck, you whey-faced sheep!" Carcolo smote the air with his fist. "I will crush you like a clod of dry moss!" He frowned, rubbed his round red chin. "But how? Where? He has every advantage!"

Carcolo pondered his possible stratagems. "He will expect me to strike, so much is certain. Doubtless he will again wait in ambush. So I will patrol every inch, but this too he will expect and so be wary lest I thunder upon him from above. Will he hide behind Despoire, or along Northguard, to catch me as I cross the Skanse? If so, I must approach by another route—through Maudlin Pass and under Mount Gethron? Then, if he is tardy in his march, I will meet him on Banbeck Verge. And if he is early, I stalk him through the peaks and chasms."

CHAPTER 7

WITH THE COLD RAIN of dawn pelting down upon them, with the trail illuminated only by lightning-glare, Ervis Carcolo, his dragons and his men set forth. When the first sparkle of sunlight struck Mount Despoire, they had already traversed Maudlin Pass.

So far, so good, exulted Ervis Carcolo. He stood high in his stirrups to scan Starbreak Fell. No sign of the Banbeck forces. He waited, scanning the far edge of Northguard Ridge, black against the sky. A minute passed, two minutes; the men beat their hands together, the dragons rumbled and muttered fretfully. Impatience began to prickle along Carcolo's ribs; he fidgeted and cursed. Could not the simplest of plans be carried through without mistake? But now the flicker of a heliograph from Barch Spike, and another to the southeast from the slopes of Mount Gethron. Carcolo waved forward his army; the way clear across Starbreak Fell. Down from Maudlin Pass surged the Happy Valley army. First the Long-horned Murderers, steel-spiked and crested with steel prongs; then the rolling red seethe of the Termagants, darting their heads as they ran; and behind came the balance of the forces.

Starbreak Fell spread wide before them, a rolling slope strewn with flinty meteoric fragments which glinted like flowers on the gray-green moss. To all sides rose majestic peaks, snow blazing white in the clear morning light: Mount Gethron, Mount Despoire, Barch Spike, and far to the south, Clew Taw.

The scouts converged from left to right, and brought identical reports. There was no sign of Joaz Banbeck or his troops. Carcolo began to toy with a new possibility. Perhaps Joaz Banbeck had not deigned to take the fidd. The idea enraged him and filled him with a great joy: if so, Joaz would pay dearly for his neglect.

Halfway across Starbreak Fell they came upon a pen occupied by two hundred of Joaz Banbeck's spratling Fiends. Two old men and a boy tended the pen, and watched the Happy Valley horde advance with manifest terror.

But Carcolo rode past leaving the pen unmolested. If he won the day, it would become part of his spoils; if he lost, the spratling Fiends could do him no harm.

The old men and the boy stood on the roof of their turf hut, watching Carcolo and his troops pass—the men in black uniforms and black peaked caps with back-slanting ear flaps; the dragons bounding, crawling, loping, plodding, according to their kind, scales glinting; the dull red and maroon of Termagants; the poisonous shine of the Blue Horrors; the black-green Fiends; the gray and brown Juggars and Murderers. Ervis Carcolo rode on the right flank, Bast Givven rode to the rear. And now Carcolo hastened the pace, haunted by the anxiety that Joaz Banbeck might bring his Fiends and Juggers up Banbeck Scarp before he arrived to thrust him back—assuming that Joaz Banbeck in all actuality had been caught napping.

But Carcolo reached Banbeck Verge without challenge. He shouted out in triumph, waved his cap high. "Joaz Banbeck the sluggard! Let him try now the ascent of Banbeck Scarp!" And Ervis Carcolo surveyed Banbeck Vale with the eyes of a conqueror.

Bast Givven seemed to share none of Carcolo's triumph, and kept an uneasy watch to north and south and to the rear.

Carcolo observed him peevishly from the corner of his eye and presently called out, "Ho, ho, then! What's amiss?"

"Perhaps much, perhaps nothing," said Bast Givven, searching the landscape.

Carcolo blew out his mustaches. Givven went on, in the cool voice which so completely irritated Carcolo. "Joaz Banbeck seems to be tricking us as before."

"Why do you say this?"

"Judge for yourself. Would he allow us advantage without claiming a miser's price?"

"Nonsense!" muttered Carcolo. "The sluggard is fat with his last victory." But he rubbed his chin and peered uneasily down into Banbeck Vale. From here it seemed curiously quiet. There was a strange inactivity in the fields and barracks. A chill began to grip Carcolo's heart. Then he cried out. "Look at the brooder, there are the Banbeck dragons!"

Givven squinted down into the vale, glanced sidewise at Carcolo. "Three Termagants, in egg." He straightened, abandoned all interest in the vale and scrutinized the peaks and ridges to the north and east. "Assume that Joaz Banbeck set out before dawn, came up to the Verge, by the Slickenslides, crossed Blue Fell—"

"What of Blue Crevasse?"

"He avoids Blue Crevasse to the north, comes over Barchback, steals across the Skanse and around Barch Spike . . ."

Carcolo studied Northguard Ridge with new and startled awareness. A quiver of movement, the glint of scales?

"Retreat!" roared Carcolo. "Make for Barch Spike! They're behind us!"

Startled, his army broke ranks, fled across Banbeck Verge, up into the harsh spurs of Barch Spike. Joaz, his strategy discovered, launched squads of Murderers to intercept the Happy Valley army, to engage and delay and, if possible, deny them the broken slopes of Barch Spike.

Carcolo calculated swiftly. His own Murderers he considered his finest troops, and held them in great pride. Purposely now he delayed, hoping to engage the Banbeck skirmishers, quickly destroy them and still gain the protection of the Barch declivities.

The Banbeck Murderers, however, refused to close, and scrambled for height up Barch Spike. Carcolo sent forward his Termagants and Blue Horrors; with a horrid snarling the two lines met. The Banbeck Termagants rushed up, to be met by Carcolo's Striding Murderers, and forced into humping pounding flight.

The main body of Carcolo's troops, excited at the sight of retreating foes, could not be restrained. They veered off from Barch Spike, plunged down upon Starbreak Fell. The Striding Murderers overtook the Banbeck Termagants, climbed up their backs, topped them over squealing and kicking, then knifed open the exposed pink bellies.

Banbeck's Long-horned Murderers came circling, struck from the flank into Carcolo's Striding Murderers, goring with steel-tipped horns, impaling on lances. Somehow they overlooked Carcolo's Blue Horrors who sprang down upon them. With axes and maces they laid the Murderers low, performing the rather grisly entertainment of clambering on a subdued Murderer, seizing the horn, stripping back horn, skin and scales, from head to tail. So Joaz Banbeck lost thirty Termagants and perhaps two dozen Murderers. Nevertheless, the attack served its own purpose, allowing him to bring his knights, Fiends and Juggers down from Northguard before Carcolo could gain the heights of Barch Spike.

Carcolo retreated in a slantwise line up the pocked slopes, and meanwhile sent six men across the fell to the pen where the spratling Fiends milled in fear at the battle. The men broke the gates, struck down the two old men, herded the young Fiends across the fell toward the Banbeck troops. The hysterical spratlings obeyed their instincts, clasped themselves to the neck of whatever dragon they first encountered, which thereupon became sorely hampered, for its own

84

instincts prevented it from detaching the spratling by force.

This ruse, a brilliant improvisation, created enormous disorder among the Banbeck troops. Ervis Carcolo now charged with all his power directly into the Banbeck center. Two squads of Termagants fanned out to harass the men; his Murderers—the only category in which he outnumbered Joaz Banbeck—were sent to engage Fiends, while Carcolo's own Fiends, pampered, strong, glistening with oily strength, snaked in toward the Banbeck Juggers. Under the great brown hulks they darted, lashing the fifty-pound steel ball at the tip of their tails against the inner side of the Juggers' legs.

A roaring melee ensued. Battle lines were uncertain; both men and dragons were crushed, torn apart, hacked to bits. The air sang with bullets, whistled with steel, reverberated to trumpeting, whistles, shouts, screams and bellows.

The reckless abandon of Carcolo's tactics achieved results out of proportion to his numbers. His Fiends burrowed ever deeper into the crazed and almost helpless Banbeck Juggers, while the Carcolo Murderers and Blue Horrors held back the Banbeck Fiends. Joaz Banbeck himself, assailed by Termagants, escaped with his life only by fleeing around behind the battle, where he picked up the support of a squad of Blue Horrors. In a fury he blew a withdrawal signal, and his army backed off down the slopes, leaving the ground littered with struggling and kicking bodies.

Carcolo, throwing aside all restraint, rose in his

saddle, signaled to commit his own Juggers, which so far he had treasured like his own children.

Shrilling, hiccuping, they lumbered down into the seethe, tearing away great mouthfuls of flesh to right and left, ripping apart lesser dragons with their brachs, teading on Termagants, seizing Blue Horrors and Murderers, flinging them wailing and clawing through the air. Six Banbeck knights sought to stem the charge, firing their muskets point-blank into the demoniac faces; they went down and were seen no more.

Down on Starbreak Fell tumbled the battle. The nucleus of the fighting became less concentrated, the Happy Valley advantage dissipated. Carcolo hesitated, a long heady instant. He and his troops alike were afire; the intoxication of unexpected success tingled in their brains. But here on Starbreak Fell, could they counter the odds posed by the greater Banbeck forces? Caution dictated that Carcolo withdraw up Barch Spike, to make the most of his limited victory. Already a strong platoon of Fiends had grouped and were maneuvering to charge his meager force of Juggers. Bast Givven approached, clearly expecting the word to retreat. But Carcolo still waited, reveling in the havoc being wrought by his paltry six Juggers.

Bast Givven's saturnine face was stern. "Withdraw, withdraw! It's annihilation when their flanks bear in on us."

Carcolo seized his elbow. "Look! See where those Fiends gather, see where Joaz Banbeck rides! As soon as they charge, send six Striding Murderers from either side; close in on him, kill him!"

Givven opened his mouth to protest, looked where Carcolo pointed, rode to obey the orders.

Here came the Banbeck Fiends, moving with stealthy certainty toward the Happy Valley Juggers. Joaz, raising in his saddle, watched their progress. Suddenly from either side the Striding Murderers were on him. Four of his knights and six young cornets, screaming alarm, dashed back to protect him; there was clanging of steel on steel and steel on scale. The Murderers fought with sword and mace; the knights, their muskets useless, countered with cutlasses, and one by one going under. Rearing on hind legs the Murderer corporal hacked down at Joaz, who desperately fended off the blow. The Murderer raised sword and mace together—and from fifty yards a musket pellet smashed into its ear. Crazy with pain, it dropped its weapons, fell forward upon Joaz, writhing and kicking. Banbeck Blue Horrors came to attack; the Murderers darted back and forth over the thrashing corporal, stabbing down at Joaz, kicking at him, finally fleeing the Blue Horrors.

Ervis Carcolo groaned in disappointment; by a half-second only had he fallen short of victory. Joaz Banbeck, bruised, mauled, perhaps wounded, had escaped with his life.

Over the crest of the hill came a rider: an unarmed youth whipping a staggering Spider. Bast Givven pointed him out to Carcolo. "A messenger from the valley, in urgency."

The lad careened down the fell toward Carcolo, shouting ahead, but his message was lost in the din of battle. At last he drew close. "The Basics, the Basics!"

Carcolo slumped like a half-empty bladder. "Where?"

"A great black ship, half the valley wide. I was up on the heath, I managed to escape." He pointed, whimpered.

"Speak, boy!" husked Carcolo. "What do they do?"

"I did not see; I came to notify you."

Carcolo gazed across the battlefield; the Banbeck Fiends had almost reached his Juggers, who were backing slowly, with heads lowered, fangs fully extended.

Carcolo threw up his hands in despair; he ordered Givven, "Blow a retreat, break clear!"

Waving a white kerchief he rode around the battle to where Joaz Banbeck still lay on the ground, the quivering Murderer only just now being lifted from his legs. Joaz stared up, his face white as Carcolo's kerchief. At the sight of Carcolo his eyes grew wide and dark, his mouth became still.

Carcolo blurted, "The Basics have come once more; they have dropped into Happy Valley, they are destroying my people."

Joaz Banbeck, assisted by his knights, gained his feet. He stood swaying, arms limp, looking silently into Carcolo's face.

Carcolo spoke once more. "We must call truce; this battle is waste! With all our forces let us march to Happy Valley, attack the monsters before they de-

88

stroy all of us! Ah, think what we could have achieved with the weapons of the sacerdotes!"

Joaz stood silent. Another ten seconds passed. Carcolo cried angrily, "Come now, what do you say?"

In a hoarse voice Joaz spoke, "I say, no truce. You rejected my warning, thought to loot Banbeck Vale. I will show you no mercy."

Carcolo gaped, his mouth a red hole under the sweep of his mustaches. "But the Basics—"

"Return to your troops. You as well as the Basics are my enemy; why should I choose between you? Prepare to fight for your life; I give you no truce."

Carcolo drew back, face as pale as Joaz's own. "Never shall you rest. Even though you win this battle here on Starbreak Fell, yet you shall never know victory. I will persecute you until you cry for relief."

Banbeck motioned to his knights. "Whip this dog back to his own."

Carcolo backed his Spider from the threatening flails, turned, loped away. The tide of battle had turned. The Banbeck Fiends now had broken past his Blue Horrors; one of his Juggers was gone; another, facing three sidling Fiends, snapped its great jaws, waved its monstrous sword. The Fiends flicked and feinted with their steel balls, scuttled forward. The Jugger chopped, shattered its sword on the rock-hard armor of the Fiends; they were underneath, slamming their steel balls into the monstrous legs. It tried to hop clear, toppled majestically. The Fiends slit its belly, and now Carcolo had only five Juggers left.

"Back!" he cried. "Disengage!"

Up Barch Spike toiled his troops, the battle front a roaring seethe of scales, armor, flickering metal. Luckily for Carcolo his rear was to the high ground, and after ten horrible minutes he was able to establish an orderly retreat. Two more Juggers had fallen; the three remaining scrambled free. Seizing boulders, they hurled them down into the attackers, who, after a series of sallies and lunges, were well content to break clear. In any event, Joaz, after hearing Carcolo's news, was of no disposition to spend further troops.

Carcolo, waving his sword in desperate defiance, led his troops back around Barch Spike, presently down across the dreary Skanse. Joaz turned back to Banbeck Vale. The news of the Basic raid had spread to all ears. The men rode sober and quiet, looking behind and overhead. Even the dragons seemed infected, and muttered restlessly among themselves.

As they crossed Blue Fell the almost omnipresent wind died; the stillness added to the oppression. Termagants, like the men began to watch the sky. Joaz wondered, how could they know, how could they sense the Basics? He himself searched the sky, and as his army passed down over the scarp he thought to see, high over Mount Gethron, a flitting little black rectangle, which presently disappeared behind a crag.

CHAPTER 8

ERVIS CARCOLO and the remnants of his army raced pellmell down from the Skanse, through the wilderness of ravines and gulches at the base of Mount Despoire, out on the barrens to the west of Happy Valley. All pretense of military precision had been abandoned. Carcolo led the way, his Spider sobbing with fatigue, behind in disarray pounded first Murderers and Blue Horrors, with Termagants hurrying along behind, then the Fiends, racing low to the ground, steel balls grinding on rocks, sending up sparks. Far in the rear lumbered the Juggers, with their attendants.

Down to the verge of Happy Valley plunged the army and pulled up short, stamping and squealing. Carcolo jumped from his Spider, ran to the brink, stood looking into the valley.

He had expected to see the ship, yet the actuality of the thing was so immediate and intense as to shock him. It was a tapered cylinder, glossy and black, resting in a field of legumes not far from ramshackle Happy Town. Polished metal disks at either end shimmered and glistened with fleeting films of color. There were three entrance ports: forward, central and aft, and from the central port a ramp had been extended to the ground.

The Basics had worked with ferocious efficiency. From the town straggled a line of people, herded by Heavy Troopers. Approaching the ship they passed through an inspection apparatus controlled by a pair of Basics. A series of instruments and the eyes of the Basics appraised each man, woman and child, classified them by some system not instantly obvious, whereupon the captives were either hustled up the ramp into the ship or prodded into a nearby booth. Peculiarly, no matter how many persons entered, the booth never seemed to fill.

Carcolo rubbed his forehead with trembling fingers, turned his eyes to the ground. When once more he looked up, Bast Givven stood beside him, and together they stared down into the valley.

From behind came a cry of alarm. Starting around, Carcolo saw a black rectangular flier sliding silently down from above Mount Gethron. Waving his arms Carcolo ran for the rocks bellowing orders to take cover. Dragons and men scuttled up the gulch. Overhead slid the flier. A hatch opened, releasing a load of explosive pellets. They struck with a great rattling volley, and up into the air flew pebbles, rock splinters, fragments of bone, scales, skin, flesh, and all who failed to reach cover were shredded. The Termagants fared relatively well. The Fiends, though battered and scraped, had all survived. Two of the Juggers had been blinded, and could fight no more till they had grown new eyes.

The flier slid back once more. Several of the men fired their muskets—an act of apparently futile defiance, but the flier was struck and damaged. It twisted, veered, soared up in the roaring curve, swooped over on its back, plunged toward the mountainside, crashed in a brilliant orange gush of fire. Carcolo shouted in maniac glee, jumped up and down, ran to the verge of the cliff, shook his fist at the ship below. He quickly quieted, to stand glum and shivering. Then turning to the ragged cluster of men and dragons who once more had crept down from the gulch, Carcolo cried hoarsely, "What do you say? Shall we fight? Shall we charge down upon them?"

There was silence; Bast Givven replied in a colorless voice, "We are helpless. We can accomplish nothing. Why commit suicide?"

Carcolo turned away, heart too full for words. Givven spoke the obvious truth. They would either be killed or dragged aboard the ship; and then, on a world too strange for imagining, be put to uses too dismal to be borne. Carcolo clenched his fists, looked west-ward with bitter hatred. "Joaz Banbeck, you brought me to this! When I might yet have fought for my people you detained me!"

"The Basics were here already," said Givven with unwelcome rationality. "We could have done nothing since we had nothing to do with."

"We could have fought!" bellowed Carcolo. "We might have swept down the Crotch, come upon them with all force! A hundred warriors and four hundred dragons. Are these to be despised?"

Bast Givven judged further argument to be pointless. He pointed. "They now examine our brooders."

Carcolo turned to look, gave a wild laugh. "They are astonished! They are awed! And well have they a right to be."

Givven agreed. "I imagine the sight of a Fiend or a Blue Horror—not to mention a Jugger—gives them pause for reflection."

Down in the valley the grim business had ended. The Heavy Troopers marched back into the ship; a pair of enormous men twelve feet high came forth, lifted the booth, carried it up the ramp into the ship. Carcolo and his men watched with protruding eyes. "Giants!"

Bast Givven chuckled dryly. "The Basics stare at our Juggers; we ponder their Giants."

The Basics presently returned to the ship. The ramp was drawn up, the ports closed. From a turret in the bow came a shaft of energy, touching each of the three brooders in succession, and each exploded with great eruption of black bricks.

Carcolo moaned softly under his breath, but said nothing.

The ship trembled, floated; Carcolo bellowed an order; men and dragons rushed for cover. Flattened behind boulders they watched the black cylinder rise from the valley, drift to the west. "They make for Banbeck Vale," said Bast Givven.

Carcolo laughed, a cackle of mirthless glee. Bast Givven looked at him sidelong. Had Ervis Carcolo become addled? He turned away. A matter of no great moment.

Carcolo came to a sudden resolve. He stalked to one of the Spiders, mounted, swung around to face his men. "I ride to Banbeck Vale. Joaz Banbeck has done his best to despoil me; I shall do my best against him. I give no orders. Come or stay as you wish. Only remember! Joaz Banbeck would not allow us to fight the Basics!"

He rode off. The men stared into the plundered valley, turned to look after Carcolo. The black ship was just now slipping over Mount Despoire. There was nothing for them in the valley. Grumbling and muttering they summoned the bone-tired dragons, set off up the dreary mountainside.

CHAPTER 9

ERVIS CARCOLO rode his Spider at a plunging run across the Skanse. Tremendous crags soared to either side, the blazing sun hung halfway up the black sky. Behind, the Skanse Ramparts; ahead, Barchback, Barch Spike and Northguard Ridge. Oblivious to the fatigue of his Spider, Carcolo whipped it on; gray-green moss pounded back from its wild feet, the narrow head hung low, foam trailed from its gill-vents. Carcolo cared nothing; his mind was empty of all but hate—for the Basics, for Joaz Banbeck, for Aerlith, for man, for human history. Approaching Northguard the Spider staggered and fell. It lay moaning, neck outstretched, legs trailing back. Carcolo dismounted in disgust, looked back down the long rolling slope of the Skanse to see how many of his troops had followed him. A man riding a Spider at a modest lope turned out to be Bast Givven, who presently came up beside him, inspected the fallen Spider. "Loosen the surcingle; he will recover the sooner."

Carcolo glared, thinking to hear a new note in Givven's voice. Nevertheless he bent over the foundered dragon, slipped loose the broad bronze buckle. Givven dismounted, stretched his arms, massaged his thin legs. He pointed. "The Basic ship descends into Banbeck Vale."

Carcolo nodded grimly. "I would be an audience to the landing." He kicked the Spider. "Come, get up, have you not rested enough? Do you wish me to walk?"

The Spider whimpered its fatigue, but nevertheless struggled to its feet. Carcolo started to mount, but Bast Givven laid a restraining hand on his shoulder. Carcolo looked back in outrage; here was impertinence! Givven said calmly, "Tighten the surcingle, otherwise you will fall on the rocks, and once more break your bones."

Uttering a spiteful phrase under his breath, Carcolo clasped the buckle back into position, the Spider crying out in despair. Paying no heed, Carcolo mounted, and the Spider moved off with trembling steps.

Barch Spike rose ahead like the prow of a white

ship, dividing Northguard Ridge from Barchback. Carcolo paused to consider the landscape, tugging his mustaches.

Givven was tactfully silent. Carcolo looked back down the Skanse to the listless straggle of his army, set off to the left.

Passing close under Mount Gethron, skirting the High Jambles, they descended an ancient water-course to Banbeck Verge. Though perforce they had come without great speed, the Basic ship had moved no faster and had only started to settle into the vale, the disks at bow and stern swirling with furious colors.

Carcolo grunted bitterly. "Trust Joaz Banbeck to scratch his own itch. Not a soul in sight; he's taken to his tunnels, dragons and all." Pursing his mouth he rendered a mincing parody of Joaz's voice. "'Ervis Carcolo, my dear friend, there is but one answer to attack. Dig tunnels!' And I replied to him, 'Am I a sacerdote to live underground? Burrow and delve, Joaz Banbeck, do as you will, I am but an old-time man; I go under the cliffs only when I must.'"

Givven gave the faintest of shrugs.

Carcolo went on, "Tunnels or not, they'll winkle him out. If need be they'll blast open the entire valley. They've no lack of tricks."

Givven grinned sardonically. "Joaz Banbeck knows a trick or two—as we know to our sorrow."

"Let him capture two dozen Basics today," snapped Carcolo. "Then I'll concede him a clever man." He walked away to the very brink of the cliff, standing in full view of the Basic ship. Givven watched without expression.

Carcolo pointed. "Aha! Look there!"

"Not I," said Givven. "I respect the Basic weapons too greatly."

"Pah!" spat Carcolo. Nevertheless he moved a trifle back from the brink. "There are dragons in Kergan's Way. For all Joaz Banbeck's talk of tunnels." He gazed north along the valley a moment or two, then threw up his hands in frustration. "Joaz Banbeck will not come up here to me; there is nothing I can do. Unless I walk down into the village, seek him out and strike him down, he will escape me."

"Unless the Basics captured the two of you and confined you in the same pen," said Givven.

"Bah!" muttered Carcolo, and moved off to one side.

CHAPTER 10

THE VISION-PLATES which allowed Joaz Banbeck to observe the length and breadth of Banbeck Vale for the first time were being put to practical use. He had evolved the scheme while playing with a set of old lenses, and dismissed it as quickly. Then one day, while trading with the sacerdotes in the cavern under Mount Gethron, he had proposed that they design and supply the optics for such a system.

The blind old sacerdote who conducted the trading gave an ambiguous reply: the possibility of such a project, under certain circumstances, might well deserve consideration. Three months passed; the scheme receded to the back of Joaz Banbeck's mind. Then the sacerdote in the trading cave inquired if Joaz still planned to install the viewing system; if so he might take immediate delivery of the optics. Joaz agreed to the barter price, returned to the Banbeck Vale with four heavy crates. He ordered the necessary tunnels driven, installed the lenses, and found that with the study darkened he could command all quarters of Banbeck Vale.

Now, with the Basic ship darkening the sky, Joaz Banbeck stood in his study, watching the descent of the great black hulk.

At the back of the chamber maroon portieres parted. Clutching the cloth with taut fingers stood the minstrel-maiden Phade. Her face was pale, her eyes bright as opals. In a husky voice she called, "The ship of death; it has come to gather souls!"

Joaz turned her a stony glance, turned back to the honed glass screen. "The ship is clearly visible."

Phade ran forward, clasped Joaz's arm, swung around to look into his face. "Let us try to escape! Into the mountains, the High Jambles; don't let them take us so soon!"

"No one deters you," said Joaz indifferently. "Escape in any direction you choose."

Phade stared at him blankly, then turned her head and watched the screen. The great black ship sank with sinister deliberation, the disks at bow and stern now shimmering mother-of-pearl. Phade looked back to Joaz, licked her lips. "Are you not afraid?"

Joaz smiled thinly. "What good to run? Their Trackers are swifter than Murderers, more vicious than Termagants. They can smell you a mile away, take you from the very center of the Jambles."

Phade shivered with superstitious horror. She whispered, "Let them take me dead, then; I can't go with them alive."

Joaz suddenly cursed. "Look where they land! In our best field of bellegarde!"

"What is the difference?"

" 'Difference'? Must we stop eating because they pay their visit?"

Phade looked at him in a daze, beyond comprehension. She sank slowly to her knees and began to perform the ritual gestures of the Theurgic cult: hands palm down to either side, slowly up till the back of the hand touched the ears, and the simultaneous protrusion of the tongue. Over and over again, eyes staring with hypnotic intensity into emptiness.

Joaz ignored the gesticulations, until Phade, her face screwed up into a fantastic mask, began to sigh and whimper; then he swung the flaps of his jacket into her face. "Give over your folly!"

Phade collapsed moaning to the floor; Joaz's lips twitched in annoyance. Impatiently he hoisted her erect. "Look you, these Basics are neither ghouls nor

100

angels of death; they are no more than pallid Termagants, the basic stock of our dragons. So now, give over your idiocy, or I'll have Rife take you away."

"Why do you not make ready? You watch and do nothing."

"There is nothing more I can do."

Phade drew a deep shuddering sigh, stared dully at the screen. "Will you fight them?"

"Naturally."

"How can you hope to counter such miraculous power?"

"We will do what we can. They have not yet met our dragons."

The ship came to rest in a purple and green vinefield across the valley, near the mouth of Clybourne Crevasse. The port slid back, a ramp rolled forth. "Look," said Joaz, "there you see them."

Phade stared at the queer pale shapes who had come tentatively out on the ramp. "They seem strange and twisted, like silver puzzles for children."

"They are the Basics. From their eggs came our dragons. They have done as well with men. Look, here are their Heavy Troops."

Down the ramp, four abreast, in exact cadence, marched the Heavy Troops, to halt fifty yards in front of the ship. There were three squads of twenty —short men with massive shoulders, thick necks, stern downdrawn faces. They wore armor fashioned from overlapping scales of black and blue metal, a wide belt slung with pistol and sword. Black epaulets extending past their shoulders supported a short ceremonial flap of black cloth ranging down their backs; their helmets bore a crest of sharp spikes, their knee-high boots were armed with kick-knives.

A number of Basics now rode forth. Their mounts, creatures only remotely resembling men, ran on hands and feet, backs high off the ground. Their heads were long and hairless, with quivering loose lips. The Basics controlled them with negligent touches of a quirt, and once on the ground set them cantering smartly through the bellegarde. Meanwhile a team of Heavy Troopers rolled a three-wheeled mechanism down the ramp, directed its complex snout toward the village.

"Never before have they prepared so carefully," muttered Joaz. "Here come the Trackers." He counted. "Only two dozen? Perhaps they are hard to breed. Generations pass slowly with men while dragons lay a clutch of eggs every year."

The Trackers moved to the side and stood in a loose restless group. They were gaunt creatures seven feet tall, with bulging black eyes, beaked noses, small undershot mouths pursed as if for kissing. From narrow shoulders long arms dangled and swung like ropes. As they waited they flexed their knees, staring sharply up and down the valley, in constant restless motion. After them came a group of Weaponeers—unmodified men wearing loose cloth smocks and cloth hats of green and yellow. They brought with them two more three-wheeled contrivances which they at once began to adjust and test.

The entire group became still and tense. The Heavy Troopers stepped forward with a stumping, heavy-legged gait, hands ready at pistols and swords. "Here they come," said Joaz. Phade made a quiet desperate sound, knelt, once more began to perform Theurgic gesticulations. Joaz in disgust ordered her from the study, went to a panel equipped with a bank of six direct-wire communications, the construction of which he had personally supervised. He spoke into three of the telephones, assuring himself that his defenses were alert, then returned the honed-glass screens.

Across the field of bellegarde came the Heavy Troopers, faces heavy, hard, marked with down-veering creases. Upon either flank the Weaponeers trundled their three-wheeled mechanisms, but the Trackers waited beside the ship. About a dozen Basics robe behind the Heavy Troopers, carrying bulbous weapons on their backs.

A hundred yards from the portal into Kergan's Way, beyond the range of the Banbeck muskets, the invaders halted. A Heavy Trooper ran to one of the Weaponeer's carts, thrust his shoulders under a harness, stood erect. He now carried a gray machine, from which extended a pair of black globes. The Trooper scuttled toward the village like an enormous rat, while from the black globe streamed a flux, intended to interfere with the neural currents of the Banbeck defenders, and so immobilize them.

Explosions sounded, puffs of smoke appeared from nooks and vantages through the crags. Bullets spat into the ground beside the Trooper, several caromed off his armor. At once heat beams from the ship stabbed against the cliff walls. In his study Joaz Banbeck smiled. The smoke puffs were decoys, the actual shots came from other areas. The Trooper, dodging and jerking, avoided a rain of bullets, ran under the portal, above which two men waited. Affected by the flux, they tottered, stiffened. But nevertheless, they dropped a great stone which struck the Trooper where the neck joined his shoulders, hurled him to the ground. He thrashed his arms and legs up and down, rolled over and over; then bouncing to his feet, he raced back into the valley, soaring and bounding, finally to stumble, plunge headlong to the ground, and lay kicking and quivering.

The Basic army watched with no apparent concern or interest.

There was a moment of inactivity. Then from the ship came an invisible field of vibration, traveling across the face of the cliff. Where the focus struck, puffs of dust arose and loose rock became dislodged. A man, lying on a ledge, sprang to his feet, dancing and twisting, plunged two hundred feet to his death. Passing across one of Joaz Banbeck's spy-holes, the vibration was carried into the study where it set up a nerve-grinding howl. The vibration passed along the cliff; Joaz rubbed his aching head.

Meanwhile the Weaponeers discharged one of their instruments: first there came a muffled explosion, then through the air curved a wobbling gray sphere. Inaccurately aimed, it struck the portal and burst in a great gush of yellow-white gas. The mechanism exploded once more, and this time lobbed the bomb accurately into Kergan's Way, which was now deserted, and the bomb produced no effect.

In his study Joaz waited grimly. Till now the Basics had taken only tentative, almost playful, steps; more serious efforts would surely follow.

Wind dispersed the gas; the situation remained as before. The casualties so far had been one Heavy Trooper and one Banbeck rifleman.

From the ship now came a stab of red flame, harsh, decisive. The rock at the portal shattered; slivers sang and spun; the Heavy Troopers jogged forward.

Joaz spoke into his telephone, bidding his captains caution, lest counter-attacking against a feint, they expose themselves to a new gas bomb.

But the Heavy Troopers stormed into Kergan's Way—in Joaz's mind an act of contemptuous recklessness. He gave a curt order; out from passages and areas swarmed his dragons—Blue Horrors, Fiends, Termagants.

The squat Troopers stared with sagging jaws. Here were unexpected antagonists. Kergan's Way resounded with their calls and orders. First they fell back, then, with the courage of desperation, fought furiously. Up and down Kergan's Way raged the battle. Certain relationships quickly became evident. In the narrow defile neither the Trooper pistols nor the steel-weighted tails of the Fiends could be used effectively. Cutlasses were useless against dragon-scale, but the pincers of the Blue Horrors, the Termagant daggers, the axes, swords, fangs and claws of the Fiends, did bloody work against the Heavy Troopers. A single Trooper and a single Termagant were approximately a match; though the Trooper, gripping the dragon with massive arms, tearing away its brachs, breaking back its neck, won more often than the Termagant. But if two or three Termagants confronted a single Trooper, he was doomed. As soon as he committed himself to one, another would crush his legs, blind him or hack open his throat.

So the Troopers fell back to the valley floor, leaving twenty of their fellows dead in Kergan's Way. The Banbeck men once more opened fire, but once more with minor effect.

Joaz watched from his study, wondering as to the next Basic tactic. Enlightenment was not long in coming. The Heavy Troopers regrouped, stood panting, while the Basics rode back and forth receiving information, admonishing, advising, chiding.

From the black ship came a gush of energy, to strike the cliff from Kergan's Way, and the study rocked with the concussion.

Joaz backed away from the vision-plates. What if a ray struck one of his collecting lenses? Might not the energy be guided and reflected directly toward him? He departed his study as it shook to a new explosion.

He ran through a passage, descended a staircase, emerged into one of the central galleries, to find apparent confusion. White-faced women and children, retiring deeper into the mountain, pushed past dragons and men in battle gear entering one of the new tunnels. Joaz watched for a moment or two to satisfy himself that the confusion held nothing of panic, then joined his warriors in the tunnel leading north.

In some past era an entire section of the cliff at the head of the valley had sloughed off, creating a jungle of piled rock and boulders called the Banbeck Jambles. Here, through a fissure, the new tunnel opened; and here Joaz went with his warriors. Behind them, down the valley, sounded the rumble of explosions as the black ship began to demolish Banbeck Village.

Joaz, peering around a boulder, watched in a fury, as great slabs of rock began to scale away from the cliff. Then he stared in astonishment, for to the Basic troops had come an extraordinary reinforcement. He saw eight Giants twice an ordinary man's stature—barrel-chested monsters, gnarled of arm and leg, with pale eyes, shocks of tawny hair. They wore brown and red armor with black epaulettes, and carried swords, maces and blast-cannon slung over their backs.

Joaz considered. The presence of the Giants gave him no reason to alter his central strategy, which in any event was vague and intuitive. He must be prepared to suffer losses, and could only hope to inflict greater losses on the Basics. But what did they care for the lives of their troops? Less than he cared for his dragons. And if they destroyed Banbeck Village, ruined the Vale—how could he do corresponding damage to them? He looked over his shoulder at the tall white cliffs, wondering how closely he had estimated the position of the sacerdote's hall. And now he must act; the time had come. He signaled to a small boy, one of his own sons, who took a deep breath, hurled himself blindly away from the shelter of the rocks, ran helter-skelter out to the valley floor. A moment later his mother ran forth to snatch him up and dash back into the Jambles.

"Done well," Joaz commended them. "Done well indeed." Cautiously he again looked forth through the rocks. The Basics were gazing intently in his direction.

For a long moment, while Joaz tingled with suspense, it seemed that they had ignored his play. They conferred, came to a decision, flicked the leathery buttocks of their mounts with their quirts. The creatures pranced sidewise, then loped north up the valley. The Trackers fell in behind, then came the Heavy Troopers moving at a humping quick-step. The Weaponeers followed with their three-wheeled mechanisms, and ponderously at the rear came the eight Giants. Across the fields of bellegarde and vetch, over vines, hedges, beds of berries and strands of oil-pod tramped the raiders, destroying with a certain morose satisfaction.

The Basics prudently halted before the Banbeck Jambles while the Trackers ran ahead like dogs, clambering over the first boulders, rearing high to test the air for odor, peering, listening, pointing, twittering doubtfully to each other. The Heavy Troopers moved in carefully, and their near presence spurred on the Trackers. Abandoning caution they bounded into the heart of the Jambles, emitting squeals of horrified consternation when a dozen Blue Horrors dropped among them. They clawed out heat guns, in their excitement burning friend and foe alike. With silken ferocity the Blue Horrors ripped them apart. Screaming for aid, kicking, flailing, thrashing, those who were able fled as precipitously as they had come. Only twelve from the original twenty-four regained the valley floor; and even as they did so, even as they cried out in relief at winning free from death, a squad of Long-horned Murderers burst out upon them, and these surviving Trackers were knocked down, gored, hacked.

The Heavy Troopers charged forward with hoarse calls of rage, aiming pistols, swinging swords, but the Murderers retreated to the shelter of the boulders.

Within the Jambles the Banbeck men had appropriated the heat guns dropped by the Trackers, and warily coming forward, tried to burn the Basics. But, unfamiliar with the weapons, the men neglected either to focus or condense the flame, and the Basics, no more than mildly singed, hastily whipped their mounts back out of range. The Heavy Troopers, halting not a hundred feet in front of the Jambles, sent in a volley of explosive pellets, which killed two of the Banbeck knights and forced the others back.

At a discreet distance the Basics appraised the situation. The Weaponeers came up, and while awaiting instructions, conferred in low tones with the mounts. One of these Weaponeers was now summoned and given orders. He divested himself of all his weapons and holding his empty hands in the air marched forward to the edge of the Jambles. Choosing a gap between a pair of ten-foot boulders, he resolutely entered the rockmaze.

A Banbeck knight escorted him to Joaz. Here, by chance, were also half a dozen Termagants. The Weaponeer paused uncertainly, made a mental readjustment, approached the Termagants. Bowing respectfully he started to speak. The Termagants listened without interest, and presently one of the knights directed him to Joaz.

"Dragons do not rule men on Aerlith," said Joaz dryly. "What is your message?"

The Weaponeer looked dubiously toward the Termagants, then somberly back to Joaz. "You are authorized to act for the entire warren?" He spoke slowly, in a dry bland voice, selecting his words with conscientious care.

Joaz repeated shortly, "What is your message?"

"I bring an integration from my masters."

" 'Integration'? I do not understand you."

"An integration of the instantaneous vectors of destiny. An interpretation of the future. They wish the sense conveyed to you in the following terms: 'Do not waste lives, both ours and your own. You are valuable to us and will be given treatment in accordance with this value. Surrender to the Rule. Cease the wasteful destruction of enterprise.' "

Joaz frowned. " 'Destruction of enterprise'?"

"The reference is to the content of your genes. The message is at its end. I advise you to accede. Why waste your blood, why destroy yourselves? Come forth now with me; all will be for the best."

Joaz gave a brittle laugh. "You are a slave. How can you judge what is best for us?"

The Weaponeer blinked. "What choice is there for you? All residual pockets of disorganized life are to be expunged. The way of facility is best." He inclined his head respectfully toward the Termagants. "If you doubt me, consult your own Revered Ones. They will advise you."

"There are no Revered Ones here," said Joaz. "The dragons fight with us and for us; they are our fellow-warriors. But I have an alternate proposal. Why do not you and your fellows join us? Throw off your slavery, become free men! We will take the ship and go searching for the old worlds of men."

The Weaponeer exhibited only polite interest. " 'Worlds of men'? There are none of them. A few residuals such as yourself remain in the desolate regions. All are to be expunged. Would you not prefer to serve the Rule?"

"Would you not prefer to be a free man?"

The Weaponeer's face showed mild bewilderment. "You do not understand me. If you choose—"

"Listen carefully," said Joaz. "You and your fellows can be your own masters, live among other men."

The Weaponeer frowned. "Who would wish to be a wild savage? To whom would we look for law, control, direction, order?"

Joaz threw up his hands in disgust, but made one last attempt. "I will provide all these; I will undertake such a responsibility. Go back, kill all the Basics —the Revered Ones, as you call them. These are my first orders."

"Kill them?" The Weaponeer's voice was soft with horror.

"Kill them." Joaz spoke as if to a child. "Then we men will possess the ship. We will go to find the worlds where men are powerful—"

"There are no such worlds."

"Ah, but there must be! At one time men roamed every star in the sky."

"No longer."

"What of Eden?"

"I know nothing of it."

Joaz threw up his hands. "Will you join us?"

"What would be the meaning of such an act?" said the Weaponeer gently. "Come then, lay down your arms, submit to the Rule." He glanced doubtfully toward the Termagants. "Your own Revered Ones will receive fitting treatment, have no fear on this account."

"You fool! These 'Revered Ones' are slaves, just as you are a slave to the Basics! We breed them to serve us, just as you are bred! Have at least the grace to recognize your own degradation!"

The Weaponeer blinked. "You speak in terms I do

not completely understand. You will not surrender then?"

"No. We will kill all of you, if our strength holds out."

The Weaponeer bowed, turned, departed through the rocks. Joaz followed, peered out over the valley floor.

The Weaponeer made his report to the Basics, who listened with characteristic detachment. They gave an order, and the Heavy Troopers, spreading out in a skirmish line, moved slowly in toward the rocks. Behind lumbered the Giants, blasters slung forward at the ready, and about twenty Trackers, survivors of the first foray. The Heavy Troopers reached the rocks, peered in. The Trackers clambered above, searching for ambushes, and finding none, signaled back. With great caution the Heavy Troopers entered the Jambles, necessarily breaking formation. Twenty feet they advanced, fifty feet, a hundred feet. Emboldened, the vengeful Trackers sprang forward over the rocks, and up surged the Termagants.

Screaming and cursing, the Trackers scrambled back pursued by the dragons. The Heavy Troopers recoiled, then swung up their weapons, fired, and two Termagants were struck under the lower armpits, their most vulnerable spot. Floundering, they tumbled down among the rocks. Others, maddened, jumped squarely down upon the Troopers. There was roaring, squealing, cries of shock and pain. The Giants lumbered up, and grinning vastly plucked away the Termagants, wrenched off their heads, flung them high over the rocks. Those Termagants who were able scuttled back, leaving half a dozen Heavy Troopers wounded, two with their throats torn open.

Again the Heavy Troopers moved forward, with the Trackers reconnoitering above, but more warily. The Trackers froze, yelled a warning, the Heavy Troopers stopped short, calling to each other, swinging their guns nervously. Overhead the Trackers scrambled back, and through the rocks, over the rocks, came dozens of Fiends and Blue Horrors. The Heavy Troopers, grimacing dourly, fired their pistols; and the air reeked with the stench of burning scale, exploded viscera. The dragons surged in upon the men, and now began a terrible battle among the rocks, with the pistols, the maces, even the swords useless for lack of room. The Giants lumbered forward and in turn were attacked by Fiends. Astonished, the idiotic grins faded from their faces; they hopped awkwardly back from the steel-weighted tails, but among the rocks the Fiends were also at a disadvantage, their steel balls clattering and jarring away from rock more often than flesh.

The Giants, recovering, discharged their chest projectors into the melee; Fiends were torn apart as well as Blue Horrors and Heavy Troopers, the Giants making no distinction.

Over the rocks came another wave of dragons—Blue Horrors. They slid down on the heads of the Giants, clawing, stabbing, tearing. In a frenzy the Giants tore at the creatures, flung them to the ground, stamped on them, and the Heavy Troopers burnt them with their pistols.

From nowhere, for no reason, there came a lull. Ten seconds, fifteen seconds passed, with no sound but whimpering and moaning from wounded dragons and men. A sense of imminence weighed the air, and here came the Juggers, looming through the passages. For a brief period Giants and Juggers looked each other face to face. Then Giants groped for their blast projectors, while Blue Horrors sprang down once more, grappling the Giant arms. The Juggers stumped quickly forward. Dragon brachs grappled Giant arms; bludgeons and maces swung, dragon armor and man armor crushed and ground apart. Man and dragon tumbled over and over, ignoring pain, shock, mutilation.

The struggle became quiet; sobbing and wheezing replaced the roars, and presently eight Juggers, superior in mass and natural armament, staggered away from eight destroyed Giants.

The Troopers meanwhile had drawn together, standing back to back in clots. Step by step, burning with heat beams the screaming Horrors, Termagants and Fiends who lunged after them, they retreated toward the valley floor, and finally won free of the rocks. The pursuing Fiends, anxious to fight in the open, sprang into their midst, while from the flanks came Long-horned Murderers and Striding Murderers. In a spirit of reckless jubilation, a dozen men riding Spiders, carrying blast cannon taken from the fallen Giants, charged the Basics and Weaponeers,

115

who waited beside the rather casual emplacement of three-wheeled weapons. The Basics, without shame, jerked their man-mounts around and fled toward the black ship. The Weaponeers swiveled their mechanisms, aimed, discharged bursts of energy. One man fell, two men, three men—then the others were among the Weaponeers, who were soon hacked to pieces, including the persuasive individual who had served as envoy.

Several of the men, whooping and hooting, set out in chase of the Basics, but the human mounts, springing along like monstrous rabbits, carried the Basics as fast as the Spiders carried the men. From the Jambles came a horn signal; the mounted men halted, wheeled back. The entire Banbeck force turned and retreated full speed into the Jambles.

The Troopers stumbled a few defiant steps in pursuit, then halted in sheer fatigue. Of the original three squads, not enough men to make up a single squad survived. The eight Giants had perished, all Weaponeers and almost the entire group of Trackers. The Banbeck forces gained the Jambles with seconds only to spare. From the black ship came a volley of explosive pellets, to shatter the rocks at the spot where they had disappeared.

On a wind-polished cape of rock above Banbeck Vale Ervis Carcolo and Bast Givven had watched the battle. The rocks hid the greater part of the fighting; the cries and clangor rose faint and tinny, like insect noise. There would be the glint of a dragon scale,

116

glimpses of running men, the shadow and flicker of movement, but not until the mangled forces of the Basics staggered forth did the outcome of the battle reveal itself. Carcolo shook his head in sour bewilderment. "The crafty devil, Joaz Banbeck! He's turned them back, he's slaughtered their best!"

"It would appear," said Bast Givven, "that dragons armed with fangs, swords and steel balls are more effective than men with guns and heat beams—at least in close quarters."

Carcolo grunted. "I might have done as well myself, under like circumstances." He turned Bast Givven a waspish glance. "Do you not agree?"

"Certainly. Beyond all question."

"Of course," Carcolo went on, "I had not the advantage of preparation. The Basics surprised me, but Joaz Banbeck labored under no such handicap." He looked back down into Banbeck Vale, where the Basic ship was bombarding the Jambles, shattering rocks into splinters. "Do they plan to blast the Jambles out of the valley? In which case, of course, Joaz Banbeck would have no further refuge. Their strategy is clear. And as I suspected: reserve forces!"

Another thirty Troopers had marched down the ramp to stand immobile in the trampled field before the ship.

Carcolo pounded his fist into his palm. "Bast Givven, listen now, listen carefully! For it is in our power to do a great deed, to reverse our fortunes! Notice Clybourne Crevasse, how it opens into the Vale, directly behind the Basic ship."

"Your ambition will yet cost us our lives."

Carcolo laughed. "Come, Givven, how many times does a man die? What better way to lose a life than in the pursuit of glory?"

Bast Givven turned, surveyed the meager remnants of the Happy Valley army. "We could win glory by trouncing a dozen sacerdotes. Flinging ourselves upon a Basic ship is hardly needful."

"Nevertheless," said Ervis Carcolo, "that is how it must be. I ride ahead, you marshal the forces and follow. We meet at the head of Clybourne Crevasse on the west edge of the Vale!"

CHAPTER 11

STAMPING HIS FEET, muttering nervous curses, Ervis Carcolo waited at the head of Clybourne Crevasse. Unlucky chance after chance paraded before his imagination. The Basics might surrender to the difficulties of Banbeck Vale and depart. Joaz Banbeck might attack across the open fields to save Banbeck Village from destruction and so destroy himself. Bast Givven might be unable to control the disheartened men and mutinous dragons of Happy Valley. Any of these situations might occur; any would expunge Carcolo's dreams of glory and leave him a broken man. Back and forth he paced the scarred granite; every few seconds he peered down into Banbeck

Vale; every few seconds he turned to scan the bleak skylines for the dark shapes of his dragons, the taller silhouettes of his men.

Beside the Basic ship waited a scanty two squads of Heavy Troopers—those who had survived the original attack and the reserves. They squatted in silent groups, watching the leisurely destruction of Banbeck Village. Fragment by fragment, the spires, towers and cliffs which had housed the Banbeck folk cracked off, slumped down into an ever-growing mound of rubble. An even heavier barrage poured against the Jambles. Boulders broke like eggs; rock splinters drifted down the valley.

A half hour passed. Ervis Carcolo seated himself glumly on a rock.

A jingle, the pad of feet. Carcolo bounded to his feet. Winding across the skyline came the sorry remnants of his forces, the men dispirited, the Termagants surly and petulant, a mere handful each of Fiends, Blue Horrors and Murderers.

Carcolo's shoulders sagged. What could be accomplished with a force so futile as this? He took a deep breath. Show a brave front! Never say die! He assumed his bluffest mien. Stepping forward, he cried out, "Men, dragons! Today we have known defeat, but the day is not over. The time of redemption is at hand; we shall revenge ourselves on both the Basics and Joaz Banbeck!" He searched the faces of his men, hoping for enthusiasm. They looked back at him without interest. The dragons, their understanding less complete, snorted softly, hissed and whispered. "Men and dragons!" bawled Carcolo. "You ask me, how shall we achieve these glories? I answer, follow where I lead! Fight where I fight! What is death to us, with our valley despoiled?"

Again he inspected his troops, once more finding only listlessness and apathy. Carcolo stifled the roar of frustration which rose into his throat, and turned away. "Advance!" he called gruffly over his shoulder. Mounting his drooping Spider, he set off down Clybourne Crevasse.

The Basic ship pounded the Jambles and Banbeck Village with equal vehemence. From a vantage on the west rim of the valley Joaz Banbeck watched the blasting of corridor after familiar corridor. Apartments and halls hewn earnestly from the rock, carved, tooled, polished across the generations—all opened, destroyed, pulverized. Now the target became that spire which contained Joaz Banbeck's private apartments, with his study, his workroom, the Banbeck reliquarium.

Joaz clenched and unclenched his fists, furious at his own helplessness. The goal of the Basics was clear. They intended to destroy Banbeck Vale, to exterminate as completely as possible the men of Aerlith, and what could prevent them? Joaz studied the Jambles. The old talus had been splintered away almost to the sheer face of the cliff. Where was the opening into the Great Hall of the sacerdotes? His farfetched hypotheses were diminishing to futility. Another hour would see the utter devastation of Banbeck Village.

Joaz tried to control a sickening sense of frustration. How to stop the destruction? He forced himself to calculate. Clearly, an attack across the valley floor was equivalent to suicide. But behind the black ship opened a ravine similar to that in which Joaz stood concealed: Clybourne Crevasse. The ship's entry gaped wide, Heavy Troopers squatted listlessly to the side. Joaz shook his head with a sour grimace. Inconceivable that the Basics could neglect so obvious a threat.

Still—in their arrogance might they not overlook the possibility of so insolent an act?

Indecision tugged Joaz forward and backward. And now a barrage of explosive pellets split open the spire which housed his apartments. The reliquarium, the ancient trove of the Banbeck's, was about to be destroyed. Joaz made a blind gesture, jumped to his feet, called the closest of his dragon masters. "Assemble the Murderers, three squads of Termagants, two dozen Blue Horrors, ten Fiends, all the riders. We climb to Banbeck Verge, we descend Clybourne Crevasse, we attack the ship."

The dragon master departed; Joaz gave himself to gloomy contemplation. If the Basics intended to draw him into a trap, they were about to succeed.

The dragon master returned. "The force is assembled."

"We ride."

Up the ravine surged men and dragons, emerging upon Banbeck Verge. Swinging south, they came to the head of Clybourne Crevasse.

A knight at the head of the column suddenly signaled a halt. When Joaz approached he pointed out marks on the floor of the crevasse. "Dragons and men have passed here recently."

Joaz studied the tracks. "Heading down the crevasse."

"Yes."

Joaz dispatched a party of scouts who presently came galloping wildly back. "Ervis Carcolo, with men and dragons, is attacking the ship!"

Joaz wheeled his Spider, plunged headlong down the dim passage, followed by his army.

Outcries and screams of battle reached their ears as they approached the mouth of the crevasse. Busting out on the valley floor Joaz came upon a scene of desperate carnage, with dragon and Heavy Trooper hacking, stabbing, burning, blasting. Where was Ervis Carcolo? Joaz recklessly rode to look into the entry port which hung wide. Ervis Carcolo then had forced his way into the ship. A trap? Or had he effectuated Joaz's own plan of seizing the ship? What of the Heavy Troopers? Would the Basics sacrifice forty warriors to capture a handful of men? Unreasonable—but now the Heavy Troopers were holding their own. They had formed a phalanx, they now concentrated the energy of their weapons on those dragons who yet opposed them. A trap? If so, it was sprung—unless Ervis Carcolo already had captured the ship. Joaz rose in his saddle, signaled his company. "Attack!"

The Heavy Troopers were doomed. Striding Murderers hewed from above, Long-horned Murderers thrust from below, Blue Horrors pinched, clipped, dismembered. The battle was done, but Joaz, with men and Termagants, had already charged up the ramp. From within came the hum and throb of power, and also human sounds—cries, shouts of fury.

The sheer ponderous bulk struck at Joaz; he stopped short, peered uncertainly into the ship. Behind him his men waited, muttering under their breath. Joaz asked himself, "Am I as brave as Ervis Carcolo? What is bravery, in any case? I am completely afraid. I dare not enter, I dare not stay outside." He put aside all caution, rushed forward, followed by his men and a horde of scuttling Termagants.

Even as Joaz entered the ship he knew Ervis Carcolo had not succeeded; above him the guns still sang and hissed. Joaz's apartments splintered apart. Another tremendous volley struck into the Jambles, laying bare the naked stone of the cliff, and what was hitherto hidden—the edge of a tall opening.

Joaz, inside the ship, found himself in an antechamber. The inner port was closed. He sidled forward, peered through a rectangular pane into what seemed a lobby or staging chamber. Ervis Carcolo and his knights crouched against the far wall, casually guarded by about twenty Weaponeers. A group of Basics rested in an alcove to the side, relaxed, quiet, their attitude one of contemplation.

Carcolo and his men were not completely subdued; as Joaz watched Carcolo lunged furiously forward. A purple crackle of energy punished him, hurled him back against the wall.

From the alcove one of the Basics, staring across the inner chamber took note of Joaz Banbeck; he flicked out with his brach, touched a rod. An alarm whistle sounded, the outer port slid shut. A trap? An emergency process? The result was the same. Joaz motioned to four men, heavily burdened. They came forward, kneeled, placed on the deck four of the blast cannon which the Giants had carried into the Jambles. Joaz swung his arm. Cannon belched; metal creaked, melted; acrid odors permeated the room. The hole was still too small. "Again!" The cannon flamed; the inner port vanished. Into the gap sprang Weaponeers, firing their energy guns. Purple fire cut into the Banbeck ranks. Men curled, twisted, wilted, fell with clenched fingers and contorted faces. Before the cannon could respond, red-scaled shapes scuttled forward. Termagants. Hissing and wailing they swarmed over the Weaponeers, on into the staging chamber. In front of the alcove occupied by the Basics they stopped short as if in astonishment. The men crowding after fell silent: even Carcolo watched in fascination. Basic stock confronted its derivative, each seeing in the other its caricature. The Termagants crept forward with sinister deliberation; the Basics waved their brachs, whistled, fluted. The Termagants scuttled forward, sprang into the alcove. There was a horrid tumbling and croaking; Joaz, sickened at some elementary level, was forced to look away.

The struggle was soon over; there was silence in the alcove. Joaz turned to examine Ervis Carcolo, who stared back, rendered inarticulate by anger, humiliation, pain and fright.

Finally, finding his voice Carcolo made an awkward gesture of menace and fury. "Be off with you," he croaked. "I claim this ship. Unless you would lie in your own blood, leave me to my conquest!"

Joaz snorted contemptuously, turned his back on Carcolo, who sucked in his breath, and with a whispered curse, lurched forward. Bast Givven seized him, drew him back. Carcolo struggled, Givven talked earnestly into his ear, and Carcolo at last relaxed, half-weeping.

Joaz meanwhile examined the chamber. The walls were blank, gray; the deck was covered with resilient black foam. There was no obvious illumination, but light was everywhere, exuding from the walls. The air chilled the skin, and smelled unpleasantly acrid. There was an odor which Joaz had not previously noticed. He coughed, his eardrums rang. A frightening suspicion became certainty; on heavy legs he lunged for the port, beckoning to his troops. "Outside, they poison us!" He stumbled out on the ramp, gulped fresh air; his men and Termagants followed, and then in a stumbling rush came Ervis Carcolo and his men. Under the hulk of the great ship the group stood gasping, tottering on limp legs, eyes dim and swimming.

Above them, oblivious or careless of their presence, the ship's guns sent forth another barrage. The spire housing Joaz's apartments tottered, collapsed; the Jambles were no more than a heap of rock splinters drifting into a high arched opening. Inside the opening Joaz glimpsed a dark shape, a glint, a shine, a structure—Then he was distracted by an ominous sound at his back. From a port at the other end of the ship, a new force of Heavy Troopers had alighted —three new squads of twenty men each, accompanied by a dozen Weaponeers with four of the rolling projectors.

Joaz sagged back in dismay. He glanced along his troops; they were in no condition either to attack or defend. A single alternater remained. Flight. "Make for Clybourne Crevasse," he called thickly.

Stumbling, lurching, the remnants of the two armies fled under the brow of the great black ship. Behind them Heavy Troopers swung smartly forward, but without haste.

Rounding the ship, Joaz stopped short. In the mouth of Clybourne Crevasse waited a fourth squad of Heavy Troopers, with another Weaponeer and his weapon.

Joaz looked to right and left, up and down the valley. Which way to run, where to turn? The Jambles? They were nonexistent. Motion, slow and ponderous, on the opening previously concealed by tumbled rock caught his attention. A dark object moved forth; a shutter drew back, a bright disk glittered. Almost instantly a pencil of milky blue radiance lanced at, into, through the end disk of the Basic ship. Within, tortured machinery whined, simultaneously up and down the scale, to inaudibility at either end. The luster of the end disks vanished; they became gray, dull; the whisper of power and life previously pervading the ship gave way to dead quiet; the ship itself was dead, and its mass, suddenly unsupported, crushed groaning into the ground.

The Heavy Troopers gazed up in consternation at the hulk which had brought them to Aerlith. Joaz, taking advantage of their indecision, called, "Retreat! North—up the valley!"

The Heavy Troopers doggedly followed; the Weaponeers however cried out an order to halt. They emplaced their weapons, brought them to bear on the cavern behind the Jambles. Within the opening naked shapes moved with frantic haste; there was slow shifting of massive machinery, a change of lights and shadows, and the milky blue shaft of radiance struck forth once more. It flicked down; Weaponeers, weapons, two-thirds of the Heavy Troopers vanished like moths in a furnace. The surviving Heavy Troopers halted, retreated uncertainly toward the ship.

In the mouth of Clybourne Crevasse waited the remaining squad of Heavy Troopers. The single Weaponeer crouched over his three-wheeled mechanism. With fateful care he made his adjustments; within the dark opening the naked sacerdotes worked furiously, thrusting, wedging, the strain of their sinews and hearts and minds communicating itself to every man in the valley. The shaft of milky-blue light sprang forth, but too soon. It melted the rock a hundred yards south of Clybourne Crevasse, and

127

now from the Weaponeer's gun came a splash of orange and green flame. Seconds later the mouth of the sacerdotes' cavern erupted. Rocks, bodies, fragments of metal, glass, rubber arched through the air.

The sound of the explosion reverberated through the valley. And the dark object in the cavern was destroyed, was no more than tatters and shreds of metal.

Joaz took three deep breaths, throwing off the effects of the narcotic gas by sheer power of will. He signaled to his Murderers. "Charge, kill!"

The Murderers loped forward; the Heavy Troopers threw themselves flat, aimed their weapons, but soon died. In the mouth of Clybourne Crevasse the final squad of Troopers charged wildly forth, to be instantly attacked by Termagants and Blue Horrors who had sidled along the face of the cliff. The Weaponeer was gored by a Murderer; there was no further resistance in the valley, and the ship lay open to attack.

Joaz led the way back up the ramp, through the entry into the now dim staging-chamber. The blast cannon captured from the Giants lay where his men had dropped them.

Three portals led from the chamber, and these were swiftly burned down. The first revealed a spiral ramp; the second, a long empty hall lined with tiers of bunks; the third, a similar hall in which the bunks were occupied. Pale faces peered from the tiers, pallid hands flickered. Up and down the central corridor marched squat matrons in gray gowns. Ervis

Carcolo rushed forward, buffeting the matrons to the deck, peering into the bunks. "Outside," he bellowed. "You are rescued, you are saved. Outside quickly, while there is opportunity."

But there was only meager resistance to overcome from a half dozen Weaponeers and Trackers, none whatever from twenty Mechanics—these, short thin men with sharp features and dark hair—and none from the sixteen remaining Basics, and all were marched off the ship as prisoners.

CHAPTER 12

QUIET FILLED the valley floor, the silence of exhaustion. Men and dragons sprawled in the trampled fields; the captives stood in a dejected huddle behind the ship. Occasionally an isolated sound came to emphasize the silence—the creak of cooling metal within the ship, the fall of a loose rock from the shattered cliffs; an occasional murmur from the liberated Happy Valley folk, who sat in a group apart from the surviving warriors.

Ervis Carcolo alone seemed restless. For a space he stood with his back to Joaz, slapping his thigh with his scabbard tassel. He contemplated the sky where Skene, a dazzling atom, hung close over the western cliffs, then turned, studied the shattered gap at the north of the valley, filled with the twisted re-

129

mains of the sacerdotes' construction. He gave his thigh a final slap, looking toward Joaz Banbeck, turned to stalk through the huddle of Happy Valley folk, making brusque motions of no particular significance, pausing here and there to harangue or cajole, apparently attempting to instill spirit and purpose into his defeated people.

In this purpose he was unsuccessful, and presently he swung sharply about, marched across the field to where Joaz Banbeck lay outstretched. Carcolo stared down. "Well then," he said bluffly, "the battle is over, the ship is won."

Joaz raised himself up on one elbow. "True."

"Let us have no misunderstanding on one point," said Carcolo. "Ship and contents are mine. An ancient rule defines the rights of him who is first to attack. On this rule I base my claim."

Joaz looked up in surprise, and seemed almost amused. "By a rule even more ancient, I have already assumed possession."

"I dispute this assertion," said Carcolo hotly. "Who—"

Joaz held up his hand warily. "Silence, Carcolo! You are alive now only because I am sick of blood and violence. Do not test my patience!"

Carcolo turned away, twitching his scabbard tassel with restrained fury. He looked up the valley, turned back to Joaz. "Here come the sacerdotes, who in fact demolished the ship. I remind you of my proposal, by which we might have prevented this destruction and slaughter."

Joaz smiled. "You made your proposal only two days ago. Further, the sacerdotes possess no weapons."

Carcolo stared as if Joaz had taken leave of his wits. "How, then, did they destroy the ship?"

Joaz shrugged. "I can only make conjectures."

Carcolo asked sarcastically, "And what direction do these conjectures lead?"

"I wonder if they had constructed the frame of a spaceship. I wonder if they turned the propulsion beam against the Basic ship."

Carcolo pursed his mouth dubiously. "Why should the sacerdotes build themselves a spaceship?"

"The Demie approaches. Why do you not put your question to him?"

"I will do so," said Carcolo with dignity.

But the Demie, followed by four younger sacerdotes and walking with the air of a man in a dream, passed without speaking.

Joaz rose to his knees, watched after him. The Demie apparently planned to mount the ramp and enter the ship. Joaz jumped to his feet, followed, barred the way to the ramp. Politely he asked, "What do you seek, Demie?"

"I seek to board the ship."

"To what end? I ask, of course, from sheer curiosity."

The Demie inspected him a moment without reply. His face was haggard and tight; his eyes gleamed like frost-stars. Finally he replied, in a voice hoarse with emotion. "I wish to determine if the ship can be repaired."

Joaz considered a moment, then spoke in a gentle rational voice. "The information can be of little interest to you. Would the sacerdotes place themselves so completely under my command?"

"We obey no one."

"In that case, I can hardly take you with me when I leave."

The Demie swung around, and for a moment seemed as if he would walk away. His eyes fell on the shattered opening at the end of the vale, and he turned back. He spoke, not in the measured voice of a sacerdote, but in a burst of grief and fury. "This is your doing, you preen yourself, you count yourself resourceful and clever; you forced us to act, and thereby violate ourselves and our dedication!"

Joaz nodded, with a faint grim smile. "I knew the opening must lie behind the Jambles; I wondered if you might be building a spaceship; I hoped that you might protect yourselves against the Basics, and so serve my purposes. I admit your charges. I used you and your construction as a weapon, to save myself and my people. Did I do wrong?"

"Right or wrong—who can weigh? You wasted our effort across more than eight hundred Aerlith years. You destroyed more than you can ever replace."

"I destroyed nothing, Demie. The Basics destroyed your ship. If you had cooperated with us in the defense of Banbeck Vale this disaster would have never occurred. You chose neutrality, you thought yourselves immune from our grief and pain. As you see, such is not the case."

"And meanwhile our labor of eight hundred and twelve years goes for naught."

Joaz asked with feigned innocence, "Why did you need a spaceship? Where do you plan to travel?"

The Demie's eyes burst with flame as intense as those of Skene. "When the race of men is gone, then we go abroad. We move across the galaxy, we repopulate the terrible old worlds, and the new Universal history starts from that day, with the past wiped clean as if it never existed. If the grephs destroy you, what is it to us? We await only the death of the last man in the universe."

"Do you not consider yourselves men?"

"We are as you know us—above-men."

At Joaz's shoulder someone laughed coarsely. Joaz turned his head to see Ervis Carcolo. "'Above-men'?" mocked Carcolo. "Poor naked waifs of the caves. What can you display to prove your superiority?"

The Demie's mouth drooped, the lines of his face deepened. "We have our *tands*. We have our knowledge. We have our strength."

Carcolo turned away with another coarse laugh. Joaz said in a subdued voice, "I feel more pity for you than you ever felt for us."

Carcolo returned. "And where did you learn to build a spaceship? From your own efforts? Or from the work of men before you, men of old times?"

"We are the ultimate men," said the Demie. "We know all that men have ever thought, spoken or devised. We are the last and the first, and when the under-folk are gone, we shall renew the cosmos as innocent and fresh as rain."

"But men have never gone and will never go," said Joaz. "A setback yes, but is not the universe wide? Somewhere are the worlds of men. With the help of the Basics and their Mechanics, I will repair the ship and go forth to find those worlds."

"You will seek in vain," said the Demie.

"Those worlds do not exist?"

"The Human Empire is dissolved; men exist only in feeble groups."

"What of Eden, old Eden?"

"A myth, no more."

"My marble globe, what of that?"

"A toy, an imaginative fabrication."

"How can you be sure?" asked Joaz, troubled in spite of himself.

"Have I not said that we know all of history? We can look into our *tands* and see deep into the past, until the recollections are dim and misty, and never do we remember planet Eden."

Joaz shook his head stubbornly. "There must be an original world from which men came. Call it Earth or Tempe or Eden—somewhere it exists."

The Demie started to speak, then in a rare show of irresolution held his tongue. Joaz said, "Perhaps you are right, perhaps we are the last men. But I shall go forth to look."

"I shall come with you," said Ervis Carcolo.

"You will be fortunate to find yourself alive tomorrow," said Joaz.

Carcolo drew himself up. "Do not dismiss my claim to the ship so carelessly."

Joaz struggled for words, but could find none. What to do with the unruly Carcolo? He could not find in himself enough harshness to do what he knew should be done. He temporized, turned his back on Carcolo. "Now you know my plans," he told the Demie. "If you do not interfere with me, I shall not interfere with you."

The Demie moved slowly back. "Go then. We are a passive race; we despise ourselves for our activity of today. Perhaps it was our greatest mistake. But go, seek your forgotten world. You will only perish somewhere among the stars. We will wait, as already we have waited." He turned and walked away, followed by the four younger sacerdotes, who had all the time stood gravely to the side.

Joaz called after him. "And if the Basics come again? Will you fight with us? Or against us?"

The Demie made no response, but walked to the north, the long white hair swinging down his thin shoulder blades.

Joaz watched him a moment, gazed up and down the ruined valley, shook his head in wonder and puzzlement, turned back to study the great black ship.

Skene touched the western cliffs; there was an instant dimming of light, a sudden chill. Carcolo approached him. "Tonight I shall hold my folk here in Banbeck Vale, and send them home on the morrow. Meanwhile, I suggest that you board the ship with me and make a preliminary survey."

Joaz took a deep breath. Why could it not come easier for him? Carcolo had twice sought his life, and, had positions been reversed, would have shown him no mercy. He forced himself to act. His duty to himself, to his people, to his ultimate goal was clear.

He called to those of his knights who carried the captured heat guns. They approached.

Joaz said, "Take Carcolo into Clybourne Crevasse. Execute him. Do this at once."

Protesting, bellowing, Carcolo was dragged off. Joaz turned away with a heavy heart, and sought Bast Givven. "I take you for a sensible man."

"I regard myself so."

"I set you in charge of Happy Valley. Take your folk home, before darkness falls."

Bast Givven silently went to his people. They stirred, and presently departed Banbeck Vale.

Joaz crossed the valley floor to the tumble of rubble which choked Kergan's Way. He choked with fury as he looked upon the destruction, and for a moment almost wavered in his resolve. Might it not be fit to fly the black ship to Coralyne and take revenge on the Basics? He walked around to stand under the spire which had housed his apartments, and by some strange freak of chance came upon a rounded fragment of yellow marble.

Weighing this in his palm he looked up into the sky where Coralyne already twinkled red, and tried to bring order to his mind.

The Banbeck folk had emerged from the deep tunnels. Phade the minstrel-maiden came to find him. "What a terrible day," she murmured. "What awful events; what a great victory."

Joaz tossed the bit of yellow marble back into the rubble. "I feel much the same way. And where it all ends, no one knows less than I."

Classic stories by America's most distinguished and successful author of science fiction and fantasy.

Gordon R. Dickson

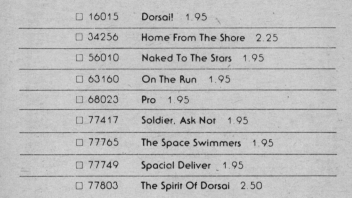

Fred Saberhagen

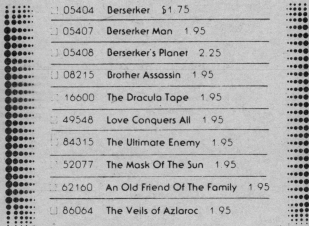

- [ ] 05404   Berserker $1.75
- [ ] 05407   Berserker Man 1.95
- [ ] 05408   Berserker's Planet 2.25
- [ ] 08215   Brother Assassin 1.95
- [ ] 16600   The Dracula Tape 1.95
- [ ] 49548   Love Conquers All 1.95
- [ ] 84315   The Ultimate Enemy 1.95
- [ ] 52077   The Mask Of The Sun 1.95
- [ ] 62160   An Old Friend Of The Family 1.95
- [ ] 86064   The Veils of Azlaroc 1.95

Available wherever paperbacks are sold or use this coupon.